Breathless With Her

Special Edition

Less Than

Carrie Ann Ryan

Breathless With Her
A Less Than Novel
By: Carrie Ann Ryan
© 2019 Carrie Ann Ryan
ISBN: 978-1-63695-409-7

Cover Art by Echo Grace

PRAISE FOR CARRIE ANN RYAN

"Carrie Ann Ryan knows how to pull your heartstrings and make your pulse pound! Her wonderful Redwood Pack series will draw you in and keep you reading long into the night. I can't wait to see what comes next with the new generation, the Talons. Keep them coming, Carrie Ann!" – Lara Adrian, New York Times bestselling author of CRAVE THE NIGHT

"Carrie Ann Ryan never fails to draw readers in with passion, raw sensuality, and characters that pop off the page. Any book by Carrie Ann is an absolute treat." – New York Times Bestselling Author J. Kenner

"With snarky humor, sizzling love scenes, and brilliant, imaginative worldbuilding, The Dante's Circle series reads as if Carrie Ann Ryan peeked at my personal wish list!" – NYT Bestselling Author, Larissa Ione

"Carrie Ann Ryan writes sexy shifters in a world full of passionate happily-ever-afters." – *New York Times* Bestselling Author Vivian Arend

"Carrie Ann's books are sexy with characters you can't help but love from page one. They are heat and heart blended to perfection." *New York Times* Bestselling Author Jayne Rylon

Carrie Ann Ryan's books are wickedly funny and deliciously hot, with plenty of twists to keep you guessing. They'll keep you up all night!" USA Today Bestselling Author Cari Quinn

"Once again, Carrie Ann Ryan knocks the Dante's Circle series out of the park. The queen of hot, sexy, enthralling paranormal romance, Carrie Ann is an author not to miss!" *New York Times* bestselling Author Marie Harte

To those who take second chances.
To those who live a second life.
To those to believe.

Breathless With Her

From New York Times and USA Today bestselling author Carrie Ann Ryan comes a sexy new contemporary series.

Devin Carr likes his life. He likes his job, his family, the outlook for his future. Then he meets her. Erin. As soon as he sees her, drunk and wearing a sequined dress as her world crashes down around her and she fights to put on a brave face, he knows what he's been missing. Her.

When Erin Taborn finds her high school sweetheart and husband banging the former head cheerleader of their graduating class at their high school reunion, she tells herself she'll be fine. She just needs to figure out what *fine* means. There's only one problem. Devin. She didn't plan on him. And for someone who thinks they have all their plans in place, that's a problem.

One she'll have to find an answer to if this whole friends-with-benefits thing is going to work.

If not, she'll fail just like with everything else.

ONE

ERIN

"OH MY GOD! YOU DON'T LOOK A DAY OLDER THAN you did on graduation day!"

"Did you see her dress? Can you say '*birthing hips*?'"

"Do you remember the time that David and Jannie got busted under the bleachers right after the pep rally? No wonder the two have like twelve kids now."

"Did you see her nose? Total nose job, right?"

"Why isn't Becca here? She probably thinks she's better than us."

"I have no idea who that woman is. Is she a spouse, or did she go with us? Why don't I remember her?"

I shook my head, holding back a smile as I stood near the punch bowl and listened to the comings and goings of people I'd gone to high school with for four years, many I'd known in middle school, and elementary before that. Time had moved on, lives had changed, and yet...it was still like walking through the hallway between classes.

A woman in a sparkly red dress waved at me, and I gestured back, but then her gaze drifted to the side. I winced. Apparently, she didn't remember me.

Yay for ten-year high school reunions.

Why was I here again?

Oh, yeah, because my husband wanted to be here. This was Nicholas's reunion too, so...here we were. In our best prom attire from the eighties or nineties since, apparently, there had to be a *theme*.

It didn't seem to matter that we'd graduated high school in 2009. Whatever. I just went along with it, though I kind of liked my red sequined dress with the slit up one thigh. It made my breasts look like they did in my early twenties.

Some people avoided their high school reunions. Some did their best to never think of them. Others tried to remember the good old days while promising themselves they would lose those ten pounds, all while writing down lists of their accomplishments so they could show the world —aka their old, so-called friends—how much happier they were, even if that wasn't the case.

As for me?

I hadn't put much thought into it.

No, that probably wasn't the best answer, but then again, I wasn't sure many people remembered me from high school anyway. I had been a straight-A student, but I hadn't spoken up in class too often. Jessica and Jackie spoke up the most. The J-Twins, as we called them, who had dated Robbie and Reese, the R-Twins.

I kid you not.

The two sets of siblings were now married and currently holding court on the dance floor.

"So, are their kids cousins? Siblings?" Jenny said from my side, and I laughed, looking over at one of the few people I still spoke to from high school.

I shook my head and hugged her tightly. "It's so good to see you! And their kids are cousins, but...genetically? I don't know if I want to do a Venn diagram."

"I've always wondered if they accidentally swapped over the years." Jenny sipped her punch, and I laughed even harder.

"We are not going to ask those questions, Jenny D."

My old friend just rolled her eyes. "Someone needs to. And I'm Jenny S. now, thank you very much. I married Tony eight years ago."

I grinned. "God, has it been that long?"

"Yup. You and Nicholas have been married for what? Six years now?"

I nodded, images of the time flying through my mind.

"Insane, right? And here we are again, in sequins and cummerbunds."

We clinked plastic glasses, and Jenny grinned. "I've never worn sequins in my life—before tonight."

"Me either. The cheerleading and dance teams did, though. But you do look fancy," I said, smiling.

"Aww, thanks, babe. I try. I don't get out much these days with the four kids and church and all of the various things kids and school bring. But Tony likes to try and take me out on a date at least once a month."

"I cannot believe you have four kids." I shook my head.

"I thought you wanted kids. I'm surprised you don't have any." Jenny's eyes widened, and she set down her glass. "Oh, my God. I'm sorry. That was the worst thing I could have said."

I shook my head, setting down my own glass so I could hold her hand. "It's fine. We decided to wait until my business was up and running, and when we were at a place where it felt right."

"Still. What if you were trying and couldn't or something? I was crass and a bitch. I'm so sorry."

"Don't be. Not with me." And I knew Jenny wouldn't make the mistake again with anyone else. Talking about the lack of children wasn't easy, and while I didn't have any for my own reasons, everyone was different.

"Jenny!" Tony called out from the dance floor. "Come dance, baby." He shook his hips, and Jenny blushed.

"I've been beckoned. It was good to see you, Erin. We should catch up again. I hate that we live in the same state and never see each other."

I hugged her tightly again, closing my eyes. "We'll make it happen. Promise. Now, go show off your moves."

"I've got the moves for sure." She winked and headed off to her husband. I kept smiling. It was good to see that people were happy now, some probably more so than they had been in school. I was, that was for sure. I loved my job, my husband, and my life. I was *happy*. Speaking of my husband, I should probably go find him. I hadn't seen him in a bit. He'd said he was going to talk with some guys he hadn't seen in years.

I waved at someone who recognized me and then headed out of the gym towards another part of the building where some other people were congregated. I passed the trophy case and touched the tips of my fingers to the glass, doing my best not to leave any smudges. There were a few football, basketball, and volleyball trophies inside.

As well as the largest cheerleading trophy in the history of the world. Becca and her girls had won state three years in a row and made sure the rest of the school knew it. They'd worked their asses off, and I'd always been proud of them—even Becca, who openly despised me for dating Nicholas.

I didn't hate her back, but we hadn't been friends either. *Teenagers*. I sighed.

I looked closer at the trophy case. I'd been on the swim

team, but I'd been firmly on the B-relay. Nicholas had been on the A-relay, but that was only because we hadn't had enough seniors to actually *have* a B-relay that wasn't just freshman who couldn't attend state.

I'd had friends, but they'd had other sets of friends who were each part of cliques of their own. I'd had a place to sit at lunch—right next to Nicholas—but we hadn't been the so-called cool table. We weren't jocks, or the drama club, or any other label that had been prominent in the day.

I'd just been...there.

I'd graduated and gone off to college with Nicholas, my equally average but decent boyfriend. Time had moved on. I'd finished university with him, and we ended up married. We loved each other, dealt with each other like any other couple who had been together since the age of fourteen. Maybe even ten if you counted when we actually met. But all in all, I was happy.

I just needed to find where Nicholas had gone off to so I could enjoy myself a bit more at this event.

"Hey, Erin! Did your sister come with you?" a voice asked from behind me. I turned on my heel, frowning. I narrowed my eyes, trying to remember who the familiar voice and face belonged to before I smiled.

"Hi, Shawnie. No, she didn't come. Jennifer was a few years ahead of us, remember? I brought my husband, though."

Shawnie came over and gave me a big hug. I winced at

how tight it was. Shawnie had been a big guy back in high school—wide yet completely built considering his position on the football field. He was even bigger now, yet still totally in shape. Back in the day, he had been part of the team that had gone to the state championship, which was a pretty big deal, since I was pretty sure our high school hadn't done it since. I hugged him back hard and then pulled away to study his face.

Shawnie had aged quite nicely. He didn't look like he'd aged the full ten years at all. His dark skin was clear of lines except for two tiny ones at the corners of his eyes—the man just loved to smile. He always had, and it made me happy that he was still smiling as hard as he was today. That meant that maybe things had been good for him. He deserved it.

"You're looking good, Erin," Shawnie said.

"Thank you for that."

"I'm just sorry your sister isn't here," he said, waggling his brows. I snorted, shaking my head.

"You always had such a crush on her."

"Of course, I did. Your sister was hot."

"Thank you for making sure I feel like chopped liver," I said, shaking my head.

Shawnie put his hands over his heart and took a staggering step back. "How dare you think that I don't find you attractive, as well. But you were always so attached to Nicky, no one else stood a chance with you." I could tell he'd held back a sneer at the name *Nicky*.

"You know he hates the name Nicky," I said, cringing.

"I think that's pretty much why we all called him that. He was such a douche about it."

"Well, that douche is now my husband," I said, grinning this time.

Shawnie had the grace to look a little embarrassed, but he just shook his head, another smile spreading across his lips. "Oops."

"Yeah, oops. But he's still my Nicholas. I'm actually looking for him. Have you seen him around?"

"No, or I probably wouldn't have called him a douche right to your face. Sorry about that, hon."

"No worries." Nicholas had been called that before, but he was still a sweet man. I was sure I'd been called worse over the years myself. Probably. "So, what have you been up to?"

"Oh, the usual. Played ball in college, though I didn't enter the draft like some people thought I would." He shrugged, and I frowned.

"I wondered about that. I didn't really follow everybody from high school. Too hard to do with the size of our class, but I did wonder."

"Never really my thing. Oh, football was always my thing. But I was good. I wasn't great."

"That's not what I remember." I was pretty sure someone had mentioned that Shawnie's running yards were still the record here.

"Well, I also wanted school to get my degree, start my

own business. Then I met Tomi, and we had our three babies. I'd rather have that than just do okay in professional sports for a couple of years before my knees gave out."

"You're married? And you have babies?" I smiled widely. He sounded so proud of those babies and his wife. And when he talked ball, it was more like he was done with it rather than like he missed it. That was good. Holding onto the past wasn't always the best thing.

"Tomi was the love of my life. Lost her two years back to cancer. But I have my baby girls, all three of them. And they are ridiculously cute. Here, I have photos."

Shawnie didn't give me time to offer condolences or even think about what to say in response to him losing his wife at such a young age. Even though he had been teasing about thinking my sister was hot, he was hurting, and I'd missed it. I didn't know what to say, but I squeezed his arm, trying to give any form of comfort I could.

I didn't know what I would do if I lost Nicholas and, honestly, I didn't want to think about it.

Instead, I looked down at the three sweet faces grinning up from the photo and just smiled wide in turn. "Those are some adorable babies, Shawnie."

"That's all Tomi."

"Hey, you're not too ugly," I teased. He threw back his head and laughed. "I'm sorry, Shawnie." I whispered the words, and he just smiled at me, sadness in his gaze. But there was strength there, too.

"Thanks for that. Wish she was here so I could show her off to everybody. But life doesn't always work the way you want it to. Anyway, I should get back, it was good to see you, Erin."

"It was good to see you, too, Shawnie."

"And if I see Nicky, I'll send him your way." He winked, and I pushed at his shoulder, waving him away as I turned to go look for my husband. I hadn't seen him for at least thirty minutes, and it was starting to worry me. We weren't always attached at the hip, but this was getting a little ridiculous. I pulled out my phone and texted him again, but there was no response. I called, no answer.

"Well, then," I whispered.

I kept walking down the hallway and spotted the bathroom, figuring I might as well do my business while I was waiting and searching for my damn spouse.

As soon as I put my hand on the door, I heard something. I didn't know what it was, but it felt off. I shrugged and pushed at the door and then froze at what I saw.

No, this wasn't a dream. This wasn't the end of a world, just the end of *my* world. This wasn't a horror show, it was just pure horror.

I wasn't standing in gray-scale, trying to keep my feet on the ground as if I were flying. This wasn't a dream.

This was real life. There was no going back from this point, no going anywhere except to watch exactly what was right in front of me.

Nicholas—Nicky—my husband, the man who had been in my life since we were ten. The one who had been part of my love life, my *only* love life, for so long. He had his pants around his ankles, his hands around the thighs of Becca, the head cheerleader, as he slid in and out of her. He grunted and panted, something he had never done with me. At least, not in years. He was always sweet with me, always gentle as if I were porcelain and he didn't want to bruise me.

He was definitely going to leave bruises on Becca's thighs.

He pushed in and out of her, his butt flexing as he grunted, and then lowered his head so he could sniff the white powder off Becca's exposed breasts.

My husband, the love and light of my life, was snorting coke off the boobs of the head cheerleader from our high school while pounding his cock inside of her.

What fresh hell was this?

I must have made a sound. I didn't know what it was, probably a gasp, maybe I had said all of that out loud. Regardless, the two of them turned to me at once. Nicky's eyes went wide, and Becca grinned like a cat that got the cream. Or the canary. Or maybe some other metaphor that actually had to do with sex that I really didn't want to think about or try to remember.

Because my husband was cheating on me, *and* he was doing drugs.

And I had no idea what to say to any of that.

Were there words for this? Was there a fucking Hallmark card? There had to be. *We're so sorry your husband is doing coke and playing with his cock in the cheerleader.* Maybe if I put enough *C*'s in the card, it'd be all alliterated and shit.

"Fuck, Erin. What are you doing here?"

He was still inside of her, his hips still thrusting slightly. Apparently, he didn't even realize he was doing it. He wiped the powder off his nose, and I just blinked.

"That's the question you're going to ask me? What am I doing here?" Dear God.

"You're supposed to be at the party," he stuttered.

"Yes, darling, you were supposed to be at the party," Becca sing-songed.

"I cannot believe I've become a cliché," I said, looking at the two of them as I shook my head. "A goddamn cliché." My heart should have hurt, it should have felt like it was splitting in two. Instead, all I could do was try to catch my breath. Try to fight through the numbness. But I couldn't. I couldn't do anything. I couldn't even cry, scream, or throw anything. There was *nothing*.

I was nothing.

I turned on my heel and walked out of the bathroom, the tapping of my shoes against the tile of the hallway echoing in the emptiness.

There weren't shouts, no screams from me. I didn't hear the sound of footsteps behind me. I didn't hear anyone following me. Because there wasn't. He wasn't going to come after me.

He would probably finish inside her, make sure he got every last line of coke.

I needed a fucking drink.

I pushed past people, and I was pretty sure they weren't even aware I was there. They were too busy paying attention to their own lives, which might not be perfect but had to be better than mine and what I had just witnessed.

My hands were shaking, and I knew I probably looked ill, maybe even a little angry, but I didn't care.

I walked out of the school, got into my car, started the engine, and found the nearest bar.

The fact that it was only five minutes away might have worried me for the school itself, but I didn't care. I just needed a goddamned drink.

It didn't occur to me until I opened the door that I was still in a sequined dress from the eighties, my hair likely in disarray. I probably looked like I was just on this side of a psychotic break.

But I didn't care. I ignored the looks, the whispers. I stomped my way to an empty barstool and took a seat next to a man with broad shoulders wearing a tight Henley.

He looked at me and frowned. I ignored him. Instead, I raised my chin and waited for the bartender to see me.

"Erin?"

I froze, knowing that voice. Remembering that voice.

I turned and saw Devin Carr. A friend from school—or at least he had been my sister, Jennifer's, friend. They had dated for a bit, not that I remembered too much about it or knew any of the details.

I just shook my head. *Of course.*

"Hi, Devin."

"I take it the high school reunion didn't go well?" he said dryly. "Amelia, my sister, mentioned it."

"Does watching your husband screwing the head cheerleader while doing drugs count as *well*?" I asked, surprised that I had even said the words aloud.

As I blinked, trying to collect my thoughts, he gave me a tight nod and glanced over at the bartender. "We're going to need two shots of your best tequila."

"I take it one's for you?" I asked.

"Nope, I had my beer. Both are for you. Figured you needed it."

And right then and there, I knew Devin Carr was going to be my best friend.

At least, for tonight.

Two

Devin

I GRINNED DOWN AT THE WOMAN IN THE SEQUINED dress, holding out my single beer bottle to clink with her first shot glass. When I came into the bar earlier for a drink after a long day, I hadn't expected to find such entertainment. But now that I had? I wasn't going to let it slip away.

Plus, I'd seen the look in her eyes, the one that spoke of pain and a manic energy that meant she could end up doing something she regretted in the morning. I'd been there before, and since I knew Erin—at least a little bit—I wasn't about to let her do something she would hate. Not that I'd let someone I *didn't* know do that if I knew it might happen, but this was a little more personal.

Erin tossed back the shot, and I took a sip of my beer, setting the bottle down after. I had a feeling I would have to make sure this one got home safely—after I got the full story out of her.

I knew Erin from back in the day when I dated her older sister, Jennifer. Jenn and I were the same age, while Erin was a little younger. I thought she was possibly older than Amelia, my baby sister, but I wasn't a hundred percent sure. All I knew was that she was younger than me. Maybe even younger than my younger brother, Caleb.

So, with the age difference, we hadn't actually been at school at the same time, but I did know who she was.

I also knew that she had married her high school sweetheart. My sister had mentioned it at some point, even though it wasn't like we'd grown up in a small town. Denver was a big place. Even if we lived in the suburbs, we didn't know everything about everyone.

However, the fact that I knew Erin had just come from her high school reunion dressed as whatever the hell she was dressed as...?

Yeah, I needed to know the story. I was nosy like that.

"Feel better?" I asked, studying her face.

She had wide-set eyes, and yeah, they had a bit of a manic look to them, but it wasn't too bad. The light green of the irises was almost piercing, and it was hard to keep focused when they were right on me. I didn't think Jenn had those eyes, and I really hadn't noticed the color of Erin's eyes during any of the times we had met back in the day.

But I was noticing now.

Though considering she still had a wedding ring on her finger—even if it turned out that he might be cheating on her—yeah, I shouldn't be looking at those eyes. Or the sharp slant of her cheekbones, or the way her blond hair was curled and pinned up on the top of her head in some weird prom hairdo.

I wasn't going to notice any of that. Or her curves.

I was just going to listen. And make sure she was okay. Because that's what I did. I made sure everybody in my life was okay.

My older brother Dimitri was the same way. We were the ones that took care of the younger siblings, even if we were a little annoying.

So I was willing to make sure Erin was okay, too. Because it looked like she'd had one hell of a night already.

"I haven't done tequila shots in far too long," she said, throwing the other shot back.

My eyebrows rose, and then I snorted, taking a sip of my beer.

"Looks like you got the hang of it, though," I said, studying her again.

"Well, I've had a really shitty night. But I shouldn't have another shot of tequila. I should probably just have some

17

water. Because I drove here. And I really wasn't thinking about what would happen next."

"If you want water, that's good. If you want something else, we'll make sure we take care of you. We won't let you drive home drunk."

"Is that a come-on? Because I'm married." Her eyes widened and then filled with tears. I cursed under my breath.

"It wasn't a come-on, Erin. I'll call your sister, or I'll get you home. Don't worry, I'm not a stranger. And I'm not going to take advantage of you. Promise."

"Promises mean shit, apparently," she said, shaking her head. "He cheated on me. He had his cock in the head cheerleader."

"The current head cheerleader?" I asked, a little worried.

She shook her head, taking a big gulp from a glass of water the bartender slid over. I nodded in thanks, and she did the same, even though she was still drinking. "No, the head cheerleader from back when I was in high school. I didn't even know that stuff happened at reunions."

"Well, people make fun of them for a reason. A lot of the old shit and resentment you thought you were over usually comes back to bite you in the ass at those things. Probably why I never went to mine."

"Well, you were lucky. Nicholas wanted to go to ours. And I thought it was because he was just tired and waiting for the next job to start and wanted to show the world that he was doing okay. But we really weren't. I mean, my work... that's fine. I own a cake-decorating business, and it's doing great. I do well on my own. Not that Nicholas has ever truly thought that. He thinks it's just a little side project. But that so-called side project paid for our mortgage. While he was always waiting for the next big thing. To sell the biggest and best property. He's still waiting for his next realtor job to pop up. Apparently, other things were popping up just fine, though. In the cheerleader."

I held back a grin at that, loving the way she was rambling. Yeah, the Rose sisters had been hilarious back in the day, and I liked getting to know them. But now Jennifer was married and not a Rose anymore. Erin was apparently married, as well—also not a Rose.

I wasn't quite sure what her last name was now. "Nicholas—Nicky—Taborn?" I asked, holding back another smile as she narrowed her eyes again.

"He hated being called Nicky."

"So you're going to call him Nicky now?"

"Maybe. I don't know. I've known him since I was ten. We were middle school crushes and high school sweethearts and a college couple, and then we were married. Everything. Married. And he cheated on me. I don't know if tonight was the first night either. Maybe this has been a long-going thing. He was doing coke, too," she whispered. "I think it was coke. The white powder you put in lines. He was sniffing it right off her boob. Like, what the hell?" She whispered the last part, and I froze, trying to picture exactly what she had seen while also not wanting to. "Jesus Christ," I muttered.

"Exactly. Jesus Christ."

"Do you want me to get you another drink? Because this sounds like you're going to need another drink."

"I shouldn't."

"I'll get you home, Erin."

"What about my car? I just don't know," she whispered.

"I'll take care of you. You want to drink for the night? You do that. You want to go home? You can do that, too. You want to go back and beat the shit out of your sorry excuse for a husband? We can also do that."

"No, I really don't want to go back there." She looked down at her dress and picked at a sequin. "They made us dress up in fashion for a decade that we weren't even in school for. I look ridiculous." She looked over her shoulder and winced. "Yeah, coming in here probably wasn't the greatest idea, considering what I look like right now."

"You look just fine, Erin," I said softly. I really wasn't hitting on her, but she looked so broken. So lost. And I had a tendency to want to help when I saw those things. I probably shouldn't, not when this wasn't my problem. But she had been the one to sit down next to me on that barstool. We had a connection, albeit one from long ago that wasn't actually between us. But I couldn't just leave her alone.

So, when she ordered a beer to follow her previous

tequila shots, I ordered a glass of water for myself and sat there as she spoke. I just tried to let her know that she wasn't alone, even if I didn't know if that was true. Because I didn't know Erin Rose, no...Erin *Taborn* anymore.

I hadn't really known her back in the day either. No matter, I hated that she was going through this.

I held back a wince as I thought about my own family and how much cheating could fuck everything up. Because as soon as someone cheated, trust was broken, and everything got messed up. Until someone left or drank themselves to death.

And though Erin had only had two shots and was nursing a single beer while chugging water, I knew it wasn't the same. It couldn't be the same as what I had seen. What I'd had to shield my brothers and sisters from.

But, still, seeing just a little bit of what had basically been my life while growing up wasn't easy. I didn't want Erin to go through this. Even if I didn't know her well, I didn't want her to go through it.

So, when she finished her beer and went to pay, I shook my head and handed over my credit card.

"I got this."

"You shouldn't. I should just call an Uber or something. I don't know about my car." She was muttering to herself, and I had a feeling she either didn't drink often, or she had a low tolerance. I could see the glassiness in her eyes, and it wasn't just from the crying. Because she hadn't cried. She'd been really good about not doing that. When the dam broke...? I wasn't sure I wanted to be there for that. But I could at least send her on her way and make sure she was okay. I hoped.

"I'll pay for this since it looks like you need it. And then I'll get you home."

"I don't want to go home," she whispered, looking down at her purse. "What if he's there? What am I supposed to say?"

I cursed. "Didn't think of that. Okay, you got my couch."

She wavered on her stool, blinking. "I don't think that's a great idea, Devin."

"I have a guest room, too. Or whatever. I promise I'm not putting on the moves. We'll just get you somewhere to sleep, and you can figure out what it is you need to do in the morning. Promise."

She studied my face for a bit before nodding, and I wondered if this was the right decision. I wasn't going to sleep with her tonight, not considering everything going on, but to anyone else, this might look weird. Or off.

I wasn't quite sure what to do. I couldn't just leave her here, and she had nowhere else to go. At least, she hadn't said so. Hadn't mentioned friends, or her family, not even her sister. So, I would make sure she was okay for the night, and then I would send her on her way.

Because I knew what happened when you were the

other person. When you had to watch your life fall apart because someone cheated. I might not be the person that had been cheated on, but I had been one of the broken pieces left behind.

I didn't know if Erin had children or anything like that. But if she did, I liked to think she would have mentioned them at least once.

However, I didn't really know her.

I paid quickly, and we headed out to my car, with Erin leaning heavily on my arm.

"Sorry, I didn't really eat today, and I don't usually drink, and I'm in heels. It's how come I'm a mess."

She wiped her face, smearing mascara. I just shook my head and helped her into the vehicle. "No worries. We've all been a mess."

"Yeah? You ever been alone in a bar in a sequined dress getting drunk with someone that you really don't know?"

"Well, I don't know about a sequined dress, but maybe a little wrap dress thing. Less sparkle."

She laughed just like I wanted her to, and I closed the door before moving around the truck to slide in.

I had an old Ford pickup that had once been my grandfather's. While it had been old even then, I loved it. My dad and I had restored it back in the day, and I had fixed it up even more on my own with some of my brothers' help over the years. I didn't take it out often since I had a work vehicle, but I was driving it today. It was one of those trucks that were good for small outings, but it wasn't in show condition or anything, so I didn't have to worry about parking or the weather or dealing with things like that.

It didn't guzzle too much fuel, and it got me where I needed to go. Connected me to some of the family that I sometimes forgot was there or tried to forget when the pain got to be too much.

And that was enough of that. Maybe half a beer was just too much if I was reminiscing about old shit like this.

"I like your truck," Erin said, looking around.

"I do, too. It's a good truck." I patted the dash and then started the engine. It roared to life, and I grinned. Yeah, I fucking loved my truck.

"What is it?"

"A '48 Ford F-1 pickup."

"Is that supposed to mean something? Sorry, I'm not really good at cars."

"It means it's a good truck. And don't worry, it'll get you where you need to go. You sure there's no one I can call for you?"

She looked down at her hands, and I wanted to kick myself for mentioning that.

"Not really. Jenn's probably sleeping. She has three kids and tends to go to sleep early these days since they all like to wake up before dawn it seems."

"Jenn has three kids?" I asked, shaking my head. "I always thought she didn't want kids."

"Yeah, that's what she said. At least when she was a teenager."

"Jenn with three kids. That's crazy."

"No kids for you?" she asked, deftly changing the subject from why she didn't have anyone to call. Maybe I'd ask again later. Or I'd just leave it be. After all, it wasn't my business.

"No kids, no wife. Been busy with work and family. But there's a lot of Carr siblings, so I'm never really alone." I winced. Yeah, I sucked at conversation.

"Nicholas and I got married right after college. No kids, though. We wanted to work on our businesses. Our careers. And I was never in a huge hurry to be a mom. Of course, I hadn't thought Jenn was in a hurry to be a mom either, and now she has three babies."

"I bet you're one kick-ass aunt, Erin."

"I hope so. I mean, the kids do adore me. And I try to spoil them, much to Jenn's chagrin."

"Sounds like she's happy."

"She is. Are you okay with that?"

I chuckled, turning down the street. "I'm just fine. We dated for like a minute if I remember right."

"Oh, but she was so in love with you."

"Yeah, teenage love, where it isn't really love."

"I used to think teenagers could really love. After all, I thought I loved Nicholas."

Once again, I wanted to curse, but I held myself back.

"I'm not saying all teenage love isn't real. And you can still have those feelings. Just because he's an asshole who deserves to be beaten doesn't mean you didn't or don't love him."

"Yeah, what does that say about me? That I could love someone who can do that to someone else. Am I a doormat?"

I shook my head, then reached out and squeezed her hand. "There's nothing doormat about you, at least from what I can tell."

"You've known me for like an hour now."

"I knew you when you were a little kid, just like I knew Nicky. You're a strong one. You're going to be just fine, okay?"

"Maybe you're right. Or maybe I need to forget, just for a minute."

I studied her face, wanting to know what she was thinking. "I've got beer at the house."

"Maybe I'll be good. Maybe." By the time I got her to the house, she was already sleeping. Probably exhausted from everything that had gone on and the fact that she was a complete lightweight.

So, I tucked her in on the couch so she could easily see the door and maybe remember where she was when she woke. I didn't want to carry her upstairs to the guest room and possibly scare her. Plus, the idea of holding her close as I had when I carried her into the house probably wasn't such a good idea. Because she had felt warm and soft in my arms. But she wasn't mine. It would be good to remember that.

I took off her shoes. I thought about helping her out of the dress, but I wasn't that much of an asshole. So, I just tucked her in and hoped she was comfortable. But she was passed out, so maybe that was something.

I went to sleep with the bedroom door open, hoping I'd be able to hear her if she moved. I knew she could call a ride share service if she wanted or needed to, but I never heard her leave. I didn't know exactly what that meant.

I woke up the next morning feeling like somebody was looking at me. I blinked open my eyes and held back a laugh —and a scream since Amelia and Caleb were both staring at me.

The two looked so much alike with their dark hair and wide eyes, but they were both holding back shit-eating grins. I had to wonder what the hell they were thinking.

And then I remembered.

Erin. On my couch. In a dress. Passed out.

Fuck.

"So, big bro, you want to tell us what's going on?" Amelia asked, fluttering her eyelashes.

"Shut up. How did you get in here?"

"You gave us keys," Caleb said, sitting at the end of the bed.

"Get the fuck off my bed."

"I don't think so. What the hell is Erin Taborn doing

here?" Caleb asked, folding his arms over his big, broad chest.

"You know Erin?"

"Yeah, in passing."

"She's really nice, but I thought she was married. I can't believe you, Devin. Do I need to call Dimitri? Because he's going to kick your ass."

"I could kick his ass," Caleb muttered.

"Of course, you could, but you're the baby brother."

"I'm still your older brother," he growled out.

"Okay, that's enough. You don't need to call Dimitri. Erin had a bad night last night, and I ran into her at the bar. So, I let her crash on my couch. Nothing happened. But the reason she had a bad night is her business. You can get the story from her if you want."

Amelia turned, and I sat up quickly, pulling at her hair.

"Hey. Watch the hair. I just had a blow-out."

"I don't even want to know what that means," I growled, sliding out of bed. Thankfully, I had put on pajamas, mostly because Erin was in the house. I was grateful that I had done that now, considering that my siblings were in the room with me.

"It just means I had a coupon and had someone else blow-dry my hair so I don't have to wash it for a few days."

"Gross," Caleb said, his eyes dancing.

"Gross? When do you shower, you ass?"

"I shower and wash my ass every day, thank you very much."

"And I shower every day, too. I just don't wash my hair every time."

"Are we done with this conversation? I really don't need to know about your cleaning habits. Now, get out."

"No, we want breakfast."

"You can make your own breakfast. I could actually use your help, though. Can you go get Erin's car? It's at the bar."

Caleb's eyebrows rose. "Seriously?"

"It's a long story. I swear everyone's innocent. Well, except for her husband."

"Oh, God. Okay, we won't pry," Amelia said, holding up her hands and glaring at Caleb.

"Promise. So, you go make sure she's awake or something because we tiptoed past. And get her keys. Let her know what's going on. And then we'll bring her car here. Don't worry."

"I'm not worried. I trust the two of you. At least, as far as I can throw you."

"With those weak-ass arms, I don't think you could throw me far," Caleb said with a grin and then ducked as I shot out my fist.

"No fighting. We don't want Erin to think we're heathens."

"We are heathens," my brother and I said at the same time, and then I snorted.

"Anyway, let's go see if she's up and get her keys. And then she'll figure out the next step."

"She will?" Amelia asked.

"I helped her for one night, but I'm not fixing her problems. Don't know if she'd want me to. I don't fix everybody's problems," I said, shaking my head.

"So you say," Amelia said with a grin. "But we'll help. I promise."

We all walked down the hall just as Erin was folding the blanket on top of the couch. Her face reddened as she looked over at us. "Oh, there's a lot of you here. Hi."

"Hi, Erin,"

"Amelia, right? I think we've worked together on a couple of projects in the past."

"Yeah, with my friend Zoey. But, anyway, give me your keys. Caleb and I will go get your car."

"Oh, you don't have to do that. I was just going to use a ride share service to get there."

"Nope, we've got you," Caleb said, reaching for Erin's purse. Amelia slapped his arm, and Erin reached for the bag at the same time. I just watched the three of them, not knowing exactly what to say. I hadn't expected the whole family to be here the morning after a woman slept at my house—when there was actually sleeping going on. Hell, what a weird night.

"We've got it. Really. You just sit here and make sure that my big brother makes you some breakfast, and then you can do what you need to do. And you can talk with us if you want. But he didn't tell us anything. I promise." Amelia was talking quickly, and Erin's eyes just kept widening. But, somehow, maybe through the magic of Amelia's smile, Erin handed over the keys and mentioned what type of car she drove. My siblings were out the door quickly afterward.

I had no idea how it had happened, but once again, I was alone with Erin. Still, there was no heat. Yeah, there was a weird connection, but it was probably just who we had been in the past and the fact that I had been there when she was at her lowest. At least I hoped that was her lowest. She just smiled up at me and shrugged.

"Really, I have no idea what's going on."

"Neither do I."

"He didn't call," she whispered. "He hasn't called all night. Not even to wonder why I wasn't home. Maybe he didn't go home."

I didn't say anything, just slid my hands into the pockets of my sweats.

"Maybe I could use some breakfast. And then I'll figure out what to do next. That's what I'm good at. Figuring out the next."

"Breakfast I can do. I'm sorry, Erin. Really damn sorry."

"Me, too." When she looked at me with those light green eyes, I wished there was something I could do to make her feel better. But I knew there was nothing I *could* do. Not just from my own experience, but from everything I had learned over the years. I walked past her and went to the kitchen. I'd make her breakfast, and then she'd walk out of my life—probably forever.

But that was good. Because she had her own problems. And I didn't need to be one of them.

THREE

ERIN

IN THE SIX MONTHS SINCE WALKING IN ON MY husband banging the former head cheerleader, I was pretty sure I'd been living an out of body experience.

Okay, maybe not an out of body experience because I was bone-deep tired, even though I was still a little invigorated at the same time. I could feel every single scrape, every sore joint, and each broken piece of my heart.

And that was because, though it seemed as if I hadn't actually been a part of it, as if I had been looking on from a distance, I had also been there.

I had gone through a divorce. Made it through splitting

up everything we'd shared for so many years, and, somehow, I made it out on top.

If *on top* meant that I was exhausted, working too many hours, and felt a little lost, then...yes, totally on top.

But it could have been worse. *Way worse.*

And that was what I kept telling myself, over and over again. I didn't know what that exactly said about me, but since it *wasn't* worse, I wasn't going to look a gift horse in the mouth.

"So, what are you doing today?" Zoey asked as she walked into the back of my kitchen, her hair pulled back from her face as she looked around. Zoey usually kept her hair flowing freely when she wasn't working—or standing in my kitchen.

I grinned and just shook my head. "Cake." I winked. "But I'm pretty sure you figured that out."

I had started Lace & Cakes soon after college. My dream had always been to become a cake decorator, even if Nicholas hadn't thought it would lead to anything.

I'd shown him.

But I wasn't going to succeed out of pettiness. I wasn't going to excel just to show my ex-husband that I could.

No, I would do it because I *absolutely* could.

If I could just get Nicholas's voice out of my head, that would help.

"You're thinking about him again," Zoey said, tapping the tip of my nose with her finger.

I scrunched my face and shook her hand away.

"I'm not."

"You are. But that's fine. You're allowed to think about him. Like cutting off certain parts of him. That would totally be okay."

I shivered.

"You really need to stop watching the ID channel before bed."

"I wasn't, I was just listening to a murder podcast."

"Okay, don't do that before bed."

"You like doing it, too."

"That might be true, but not when it's dark out. I only listen to murder when it's light out." I looked over my shoulder, making sure that a guest hadn't dropped by.

I didn't actually sell cakes at my place of business. Not in the way a bakery would. There were many bakeries in Denver, most a lot more productive and successful than I was. But mine was unique. I had a front area with a glass case that showed off a cake or two, but those were either ones ready to be taken to their new owners, or practice cakes that looked good enough to be out front but were actually ones that I would donate to a local shelter or something. Or, ones I would eat out of desperation. Not that I needed to eat any more cake, considering I'd gained fifteen pounds after my divorce. I liked the way I looked and didn't mind, but I would make sure I didn't throw myself into sugar. Even yummy sugar that beckoned me.

"You're thinking again," Zoey sing-songed, looking into the bowls of frosting.

"I'm not. And if you touch any of that frosting with your finger, that's a health code violation, and I will murder you."

"And murder isn't a health code violation? Of course, then you would be your own ID channel special, and that would be interesting."

"You need help. A lot of help."

"Perhaps. Anyway, what are we working on today?"

"Today, I'm working on a retirement cake for someone who likes to golf. So, we're going with a very large golf ball that reminds me of Epcot for some reason," I said, laughing, pointing at the very white ball of frosted cake. "And then the base is going to be a four-hole golf course."

"Four holes?" Zoey asked, frowning.

"We cut it down since we didn't want the cake to be the size of the building."

Zoey tilted her head, studying me. "Aren't they usually nine? Or like eighteen? I really should know more about golf outside of the jokes you hear at a bar."

"There are golf jokes you'd hear at a bar?" I asked with a laugh. "No, I really don't want to know what type of jokes you hear. Probably have to do with a lot of balls and rods."

"You got it in one. Hey, hole in one. Look at me, making all the jokes."

"In order for it to be a joke, I think it actually has to be funny." I ducked as she tried to punch me, even though I knew it wouldn't have been too hard. Zoey was my friend and also someone that I worked with when our jobs over-lapped. She was a florist who worked with weddings, and since I was a cake decorator, I tended to work with weddings, too. So, we joined forces when we could, and made sure our clients knew that we worked well together. Having wedding planners know that we could be a team, even if we weren't under the same business umbrella, was very helpful when it came to getting referrals and making our businesses work.

"Anyway, they also want a bunch of little cupcakes that they want toppers for. So, I think I'm going to go for the miniature golf look because they have grandchildren that love playing that. And the cupcakes are for them."

"They didn't give you an idea of what they wanted?" Zoey asked, frowning again.

I blew some stray hair from my face, annoyed that it was starting to come out of its tie. "Nope. They just said they wanted golf and would be fine with anything I did."

"I hate that. Because if you don't get it a hundred percent right, then they'll be sad. Or they'll complain. A bad Yelp review can ruin everything."

"Tell me about it," I said, going over to the sink to wash my hands again before moving to the corner to fix my hair, then back to the sink to rewash my hands. I had been working all day, knew I was covered in flour, probably some frosting, and a little egg yolk, but that was fine. I had two people that worked for me part-time but were off today because of their kids' school functions. So, I was alone and a little behind. But it wasn't anything I couldn't handle on my own.

"Anyway, we'll make it work. And if they don't like it, then I just won't think about it."

"They're going to love it. You really get the heart and soul of what people want. Even when it comes to cupcakes with little windmills on them."

I rolled my eyes and went back to mixing the frosting. "I cannot put an actual windmill on top of a cupcake."

"Well, that's the thing I think of when I think of miniature golf. Of course, now I'm picturing like the Moulin Rouge windmill. That would be great. A whole Moulin Rouge cake with red icing, and Ewan McGregor just lying prostrate, readying himself for me."

"I really want nothing to do with that imagination of yours. And never again will you say the word *prostrate* or the phrase *readying himself*. Ever."

"What? You know you've thought about it."

"Not in this bakery. This is a penis-free zone."

Zoey snorted and took a step back when I glared.

"What?" I snapped.

"Oh, nothing. It's just the idea that you think this could be a penis-free zone."

"It can be a penis-free zone. And stop making me say the word *penis*."

"Do you like *dick* better? Or *schlong*. Or *cock*. Or *meaty magic rod*. Or *pogo stick*."

"What the hell have you been reading?"

"Hey, a lot of those were from songs. And most books these days use the good words. Like *cock*. *Dick*. And *length*."

"Please stop talking about that appendage." I closed my eyes, holding back a smile.

"Dick dick dick dick dick dick dick." Zoey danced and sang the word over and over again. I couldn't help but laugh with her while shaking my head.

"You're ridiculous."

"I am. But back to work."

"Yay."

"So, I take it you're not going to make a dick cake for the next bachelorette party that comes in?" she asked, waggling her brows.

"If we weren't at my place of business, I would throw this frosting at you. You're very lucky I don't kick you out of here."

"What? I'm making you laugh. I like making you laugh. You haven't done much of it these days."

"I've been doing much better, thank you very much."

"I know. And I'm happy for you. Proud of you, in fact. But we will talk about work. I promise."

"Good." Because I didn't want to talk about what hurt. Or what I was going through. Because I had already gone through it. I was okay. I was a single woman now. And wasn't that thought fun? I had my own business, and I was doing just fine. I wasn't going to throw up thinking about the fact that Nicholas wasn't with me anymore. That I lived in a different home. That I lived alone. I wasn't going to think about the fact that the only reason I had this business at all anymore was because it had been in my name and not his. He hadn't wanted anything to do with it. Hadn't wanted anything to do with *me*. No, I wasn't going to think about any of that. But it still hurt.

It hurt that I'd had to move to a different house, as had he. Because the house we'd bought together had to be sold so it could be split up properly. I didn't want to think about the fact that I still had some of his boxes in my garage because I'm too nice and, God forbid he help clean out the place when we were packing and moving out. I didn't want to think about the fact that he was still bopping that woman.

And I didn't want to think about the fact that I kept calling her "that woman."

She had a name. And she had her faults. Just like Nicholas did. And I couldn't just call her names and be done with it. Because I had to call him names, too. Or I had to stop thinking about it altogether. That would be best.

"You're thinking again," Zoey said. This time, her voice didn't hold any laughter, there were no jokes. And I knew that what I was thinking must be clearly written all over my face.

After all, I wasn't good at hiding my emotions. Even though I tried. I attempted to be the ice queen that worked with icing, but it just didn't work out.

"Anyway, let's talk about good things." Zoey smiled, but there was a little brittleness to it as if she were trying to make sure I was happy. But that was up to me. I was responsible for my own happiness. I'd learned that the hard way. So, I'd be okay. Because I had to be.

"We have the Proctor-Jordan wedding coming up, right?" I asked, working on decorating. I had everything in my head, as well as on my tablet and computer. I liked to be organized, liked to know exactly what I was doing. Since Zoey had her tablet out and was on the app that synced to mine, I knew we'd be okay. I didn't have to stop working so I could work on something else. Yay, for multitasking.

"Yes. Now they want bright colors, not pastels. They want it so bright you can see it from space. Literally, those were their words," Zoey said with a grin.

"I remember. I think we're going for Crayola bright if I remember right."

"Oh, you remember right."

"They want it so bright, it'll sear your corneas. Again, their words."

"We'll make it work. We have the next meeting where we go over the final design for the cake. We're going four tiers and stacked. They want it a little haphazard, so not all of the stacks will make sense. And they want hat boxes rather than the traditional squares or circles."

"Makes sense. They want it bright and fun and wacky. They're a fun couple, though," Zoey said with a grin.

"Yeah, Karen and Louis have been together for twenty years now, and they're finally tying the knot."

"They had their commitment ceremony about a decade ago before either of us was in business. But instead of going back to the person that helped them then, they came to us. It's kind of nice. That we're going to be there for this new moment in their lives."

"I like that. Being part of their lives when they're the happiest," I said, letting my thoughts drift again.

Zoey tapped me on the nose once more.

"Stop it. They are going to be happy. And so are you. Got me?"

"You sure are forceful these days."

"I've always been this way. I just reined it in before. Now, I won't. Ever." She threw back her head and laughed, and I just grinned, shaking my head.

The door opened, the bell tinkling, and I looked over the glass case since we were working in the front part of the kitchen in case anyone came in. I froze when I saw who entered.

Oh, God. I knew that face. Knew that strong jaw, and those bright eyes. I knew the way that dark hair slid over that forehead. I knew those broad shoulders and slender hips and thick thighs. Oh, yes, I knew this man.

Though I hadn't slept with him, had never seen him naked, I *had* slept over at his house.

"Devin," I whispered and then cleared my throat. "Well, hi there. How can I help you? Uh, how are you?" *Smooth, Erin.*

His eyes widened for a minute, and then he looked between Zoey and me, a grin spreading over his face. It made his beard look even sexier. And since he was wearing a T-shirt and jeans, I could see the very sexy tattoos all over his arms, and a little bit peeking out at his collar.

Dear God, had I noticed those tattoos before? Oh, yeah, I had. I'd had a vivid dream or four recently about licking every single one of those tattoos. And...other things.

No, I was staying away from penises. More specifically, I was staying away from Devin Carr's penis. I didn't want a man, didn't want anyone.

I was completely fine by myself.

Just because he was sexy as fuck, didn't mean I was going to do anything about it.

But, seriously. Sexy. As. Fuck.

"Hey, there. I didn't know this was your place."

I shivered at the growl in his voice. I should not be trembling at that. Damn him.

Damn all men.

No, I wouldn't become a man-hater. But I could be a man-avoider. Yes, that sounded much better.

"Yup. I own Lace & Cakes."

"What's the lace for?" he asked, shoving his hands into his pockets. That just made me look down at the bulge beneath his zipper. I ignored it. Yup. Ignored it. Sure.

See? I was doing a great job. So good.

When Zoey cleared her throat, I figured I wasn't doing that good of a job, after all.

"The lace was because I wanted it to sound pretty, and because I do a lot of wedding cakes."

"Makes sense. Hey, Zoey."

"Hey, Devin."

I looked between them, my brows raised.

"You two know each other?"

"Oh, yeah. I work with his sister, Amelia, often. She owns a landscaping business."

"Landscaping and flowers. Makes sense."

"Just like cakes and flowers do, I guess," Devin said, rocking back on his heels.

"Yeah, I tend to work with everybody it seems," Zoey said, grinning. "I didn't know you two knew each other."

"He used to date my older sister," I said quickly.

"Oh, yeah. Now I remember." Zoey just smiled widely, putting her hands on her hips. "Looks like you lost out on that. Now she has three beautiful babies and a wonderful husband."

"Seems like," Devin said, not taking his eyes off me.

Well, then.

"What can I do for you, Devin? I didn't know you'd be coming in today. Or ever." Was I rambling? I was rambling.

"It's my friend's fortieth, and I'm here to pick up a cake."

"I didn't see your name." I wiped my hands and picked up my tablet. I would have remembered seeing his name. Not that I had a crush on him or anything. I wasn't a teenager. But he had been there for me when I needed him so, of course, I'd remember if I saw his name.

"No, his wife's the one who ordered it. I have a note from her, and instructions for you to call her in case I can't pick it up. But she was busy. One of the kids got strep throat."

"Oh, that sucks," I said, wincing.

"Tell me about it. So, the kid is going to miss out on her dad's birthday, and that sucks. But the party's still going on, and Laney's working overtime to make sure it happens. Greg's a good guy and deserves to actually have a day off just to celebrate. Even if he's going to be a bit sad the whole time because his little kid's sick."

"And you can't change a birthday or things like that," I said quickly, going back to pick up Greg and Laney's cake. I'd checked the note he brought just to be sure, but I had a feeling that Devin wasn't making up an elaborate story just

45

to steal a cake. Plus, I knew him. Sort of. I had slept over at his house, after all. That counted, right?

"Yeah, they'll figure something out. And then they'll probably have a whole daddy-daughter day since she's a daddy's girl, after all."

"That makes it even worse," I said, placing the cake on the counter. It was already in a box, ready to go. They had wanted a one-layer sheet cake with some pretty decorations on top. So, thankfully, it wouldn't be too hard to transport.

"Anyway, just came in to pick up the cake. But if there's anything else I need to do, let me know."

"No, just check it out. I would send a picture to Laney so she's good, too," I said, smiling. Zoey was being suspiciously silent, and I had a feeling she wasn't going to be so quiet once Devin left. Oh, good.

"So, what do you think?" I asked, opening up the top of the box.

Devin's eyes widened a fraction, and he slid his hands out of his pockets.

"That's fucking amazing," he whispered. "It actually looks like the ocean."

"They wanted an undersea sheet cake, so...I made it happen. The starfish and the little crab are my favorites."

"It looks almost real, and yet, fun. Much like Greg and Laney."

"They're real and fun?" I asked, laughing.

"You know what I mean. They're very responsible, do what they need to do, but they have a playful side."

"You sure know a lot about them."

"I've worked with Greg for a while now, and I've known Laney since Greg first started at the office. They're good people."

"They are. So, you're a mailman?"

"I am a postal carrier, not a mailman." He raised his chin a bit, even though I saw the laughter in his eyes.

"Well, I'm sorry. Although, I will be singing *Please Mr. Postman* until the end of time now."

"I hate that song," he grumbled, pulling out his wallet. "How much do I owe you?"

"I already have a credit card on file. If you could just text Laney and let me know if using that's okay, you can have the cake."

"Sounds like a plan. It was good seeing you again, Erin. You look happier."

I rolled my eyes, knowing my cheeks were red. "Well, considering you saw me at possibly my lowest ever, it's good to know that I look happier."

"Yeah, I'm not saying that the sequined dress wasn't hot and all, but you look better with flour on your cheek, and laughter in your eyes."

I raised my hand to wipe my face, knowing Zoey was just watching us, waiting as if she were stalking her prey. And I was the quarry she would eventually pounce on.

Great.

Laney texted Devin back quickly, saying that she loved it, and we settled the bill.

"It was good to see you, Erin. You, too, Zoey."

"Oh, good. I'm glad you remembered I was here."

"Shut up." He growled, and I just smiled, clasping my hands in front of me. See? Everything was fine. This wasn't awkward. Or weird. It was totally awkward and weird.

"I'll see you around, Erin. Bye, Zoey."

"You sure will," Zoey said, and I just raised my hand to wave, not sure what to say. After all, there really wasn't much to say at all.

So he left, and I did my best not to watch his ass as he walked away.

"You know his ass has always looked good in jeans. Just wait until you see him in shorts."

I sputtered. "Shorts?"

"You know, the shorts that postal carriers wear. Ooh, sexy man."

"He's your friend's older brother."

"He is, and I enjoy razzing Amelia about it. You know I don't actually have a crush on him." I nodded. She'd mentioned her long-time crush before, and it definitely wasn't Devin. "So, you know Devin? Tell me all. Tell me, tell me, tell me."

"Should I start with the night I slept over, or should I

end there?" I said, not knowing why that teasing sentence had come out of my mouth.

"Oh my God. He's the one whose house you slept at?" Sadness filled her eyes, and I figured whatever she said next wasn't going to be teasing anymore. Well, damn it.

"Yes, he was a gentleman, and the Carr siblings took care of me. And then I never heard from him again. It's not like I left my number, though. Everything is fine. I'm fine. Now, let's get back to work. Because I don't want to get behind."

"There was chemistry, I'm just saying."

"That's fine. You can think what you want, but I'm staying away from penises. All penises."

Zoey just looked at me, and I had a feeling she didn't believe me. Then again, as I thought about Devin's growl, and the way he filled out those jeans... I wasn't sure I believed myself.

Four

DEVIN

"You sure do know how to enjoy your day off."

I grinned up at Amelia, wiping the dirt from my hands on my worn jeans.

"I don't mind working with you. It keeps me fit." I patted my flat stomach, and my little sister just rolled her eyes.

"You are constantly on your feet, lifting boxes, dealing with stray dogs, and countless other things that you have to deal with being a postman. I'm pretty sure you do not need my job to stay fit."

"You know I'm a postal carrier, not a postman." I growled out the words, but she knew I was kidding. I honestly didn't care. I just liked saying it, mostly because it annoyed my kid sister and brother to no end. Dimitri didn't really mind. He was a little older than I was and didn't get as ruffled. After everything he'd been through...? There was no way my jokes would rile him.

"You're a dork, but I love you," Amelia said, grinning up at me before going back to the soil. We were working out back in her office's yard. Amelia liked to keep one that was like a show yard so people could look and see what she could do. She also had her own portfolio and things for people to look at, and each house would always be different, but I knew that she liked to have this done because it made her happy. She had her own house where she worked on the grounds constantly, but this was like another piece of her home.

I definitely didn't mind that my baby sister was really good with keeping things alive and watching them grow. It kept my yard and landscaping looking fucking amazing.

"You know, every time you mention what you do, I sing that song," Tobey said, rubbing shoulders with Amelia.

"That's the second time today someone's said that. And it's not getting funnier anytime soon," I called out.

"I can't help it. It's just so catchy." Tobey started singing, and I met Amelia's eyes. She was very lucky that Tobey was her best friend. Because I wanted to murder the guy sometimes. Yeah, he was good to my sister. No, I had no idea why the two of them weren't married already, but it wasn't my place to say. They were best friends, and that was just something I had to deal with.

I liked Tobey just fine, but sometimes, he was annoying as hell. Then again, I figured I was a little annoying, too. At least to Amelia. After all, that's what big brothers were for. And she had a bunch of them.

Well, three of us anyway. But I guess that added up after a while.

"So, what have you been doing on your day off today? Besides helping me," Amelia asked, using the shovel to dig a new hole. She was planting a tree, one that she would end up digging out eventually for a new house. But for now, this would be its home. One where it could grow in safety before it was ready to be fully planted. I had no idea how my sister made everything work, but then again, it was her job. Not mine.

"You know me, always busy."

"Yeah, I figured you're not one to lay around. I mean, not all of us can have every Sunday off thanks to the government."

"Yes, having exactly one day off a week is totally out of the question."

"You work six days a week?" Tobey asked, scrunching his face. "Is that legal?"

I met Amelia's gaze and then rolled my eyes. Tobey was

sweet, but sometimes, he was a little slow. Well, not really, he just took things very literally at times. And that was fine, but he didn't get my humor all the time. Or ever.

"No, I only work five days a week, but I always get Sundays off."

"I thought I saw some mail carriers working on Sundays now."

"Special circumstances, and not me. I've worked long and hard for my rest. And I'm going to keep it."

"Until you're old and wrinkly and can't lift the boxes that you need to put on the porches?" Amelia asked, batting her eyelashes. "I mean, you're already well on your way to that ancient-ness, right?"

"You're lucky there's a witness here, or I would bury you in that hole you're digging," I growled out.

"Hey, you may be bigger than me, but I can still take you," Tobey said, waving his spade around. "After all, I have a weapon."

"Aw, look at you defending me," Amelia said, grinning up at Tobey. Yeah, I saw that look in her eyes. She was going to be in a world of hurt if she didn't make a move or ignore that crush of hers. But I had already stepped in it more than once when it came to my little sister. She didn't need my help, didn't need anything from me. She just needed me to be here, so I would be. And if her best friend hurt her, I would beat his ass. After all, that was my right as the big brother. And Caleb and Dimitri would be right by my side, making sure Tobey rued the day he ever dared to hurt our baby sister.

Amelia leaned forward and punched me in the gut.

"What was that for?" I asked.

"You have that growly vibe going on. I have a feeling you're about to do something overprotective that'll annoy me."

"How on Earth can you tell that just from a look?"

"I have my ways. Plus, you just answered my question."

I rolled my eyes and leaned forward to kiss the only spot on her face that didn't have dirt on it.

"You're filthy, Amelia."

"So are you. But I love this job. I mean, look at all of this. It's all growing and pretty and green and colorful. I can't wait to start my next project, though. It's probably going to break part of my body, most likely my back, but it'll totally be worth it."

I narrowed my eyes. "Is it too much for you? Do you need to hire more people?"

Tobey muttered under his breath and winced. "Oh, bro, you stepped in it this time."

"Tobey is right, my dear brother. There's a lot of fertilizer right here, but you're the one that's standing in manure."

"How long have you been waiting to make that type of shit joke?" I grinned.

"Ha-ha. No, I don't need to hire anyone else. I have

three part-timers that come in when their schedules allow, and I can do everything else on my own. I have a strong back, and even though I joke about it, I'm just fine. I like my job. You do not need to come in here and growl at me and try to take over. Do you hear me, Devin Carr?"

"Oh, you got full-named," Zoey said as she walked into the back yard. "There's my best friend."

"Can you believe him?" Amelia asked, gesturing towards me. "He gets all growly and thinks I can't handle it. It's like I haven't built this business from the ground up. Yes, I've needed help on occasion and took it because my friends and family offered. But I'm the one who's put sweat, blood, and tears into this. Literally."

Amelia raised her chin, and I sighed.

"Don't sic Zoey on me. I'm sorry, Amelia. I was just worried that you might need to hire new people because your business is growing so much."

"Sure. I'm sure that's exactly what you meant. But I'm fine. I own my own business. I know what I'm doing."

"And because I don't own my own business I can't help out?" I asked, wondering why I felt a little hurt by that.

Amelia rolled her eyes, and Zoey went to my side, elbowing me in the hip. "You know she didn't mean it like that," she said.

"Maybe. But now I'm the one who's feeling hurt."

"You are not. You have a steady job, a full pension, and

you don't have to worry about self-employment tax. Or business tax. Taxes period."

"Oh, I have to worry about taxes. Taxes literally pay for my job."

"True, so I guess you could say I'm your boss," she said with a grin. Zoey and Tobey laughed outright.

"Wow, that would be the end of the world right there, wouldn't it?"

"I'm about to throw dirt at you, dear brother. But I don't want to waste it."

"You're literally standing on a mound of it. I'm sure you can waste a little."

"But this is my perfect dirt. My precious soil with its beautiful pH balance. I love you, my babies."

She leaned down and patted the dirt pile. I met Zoey's eyes, both of us pressing our lips together so we wouldn't break out into laughter. Amelia was a character, all right. Oh, she probably didn't always talk to her dirt like she was right now, but she liked to put on a show for me and the rest of the family. Mostly because she wanted to make sure everyone knew she was just fine.

After all, it was only the four of us now. Well, five if you included Dimitri's woman, Thea. My brother's wife was pretty damn amazing, far better than his first wife, and that meant we were a tight unit. We didn't have anyone else. We hadn't had anyone else even when people were raising us— or what passed for that in our world.

And so, Amelia needed to make sure that the world knew that she could survive on her own and prosper.

I knew that. All of us did.

I just wish there was a way to make sure Amelia knew that *we* knew. Because no matter what we told her, she didn't quite seem to believe us. But I guess that's what being a little sister meant.

Always be on the lookout for the overprotective brother. And, hey, I happened to be a very good overprotective brother.

"So, what are you doing here, Zoey?" Amelia asked after we'd gone back to work. Zoey stood off to the side, not getting her hands dirty. That was actually a little unusual since she was typically one of the first people outside of Amelia to throw herself into a dirt pile and help out. But considering that she was wearing a cute little floral dress and apron, I had a feeling she had meetings and didn't want to get dirty. After all, this was the second time I saw her today. Though I really did not want her to mention exactly where I had seen her before.

From the gleam in her eye, I had a feeling there would be no such luck.

Oh, good.

"Oh, I just wanted to come by and see you and gossip. But since the subject of my gossip is here..." she began.

"That means you're not going to talk about it, right?" I put in quickly.

"Ooh, gossip about Devin?" Amelia asked. "One of my favorite kinds."

"At least, it's not about me," Tobey said, grinning. "I mean, sorry, Devin. But it's time."

Amelia just laughed over at her best friend. I closed my eyes and groaned.

"Oh, fine."

"Well, this is the second time I've seen Devin today," Zoey began.

"Ooh, really? Where did you see him before?"

"At Erin's. Picking up a cake."

"For your friends Greg and Laney, right?" Amelia asked.

"Yep. Erin did a great job on the cake."

"And from the way Devin was looking at her, that wasn't the only thing he wanted her to frost." The two girls laughed, and I met Tobey's gaze.

"I don't even know what that means. Shouldn't I be the one frosting her?" I held up my hands. "No, I really do not want you to answer that question. Ever. Especially not in front of Amelia."

"Thank you. Thank you for not asking about frosting in front of me. Ever. And now I can never have a cupcake again. What have you done?" my sister asked Zoey. "I love cupcakes, and you've ruined them for me."

"Well, there are brownies and pies."

"No, pies remind me of that movie," Tobey put in, and I snorted.

"Yeah, I never did look at a warm apple pie the same way again," I said with a grin as Tobey and I laughed, and the girls groaned.

"You're a horrible person. Horrible." Amelia put her dirty hands on her hips and glared. "Whatever shall I do without baked goods?"

"Don't think of dick while you're eating it?" Zoey asked, and I closed my eyes. "Please, can we move off this conversation? We can talk about anything else. Just not this."

"Well, how about we talk about the sparks flying between you and Erin? Because, wow."

"Shut up."

"I will not shut up, Devin. I saw the way you two were with each other."

"So, Erin... Jennifer's sister? The one you let spend the night at your house?"

"I didn't realize it was her," Zoey said quickly. "I mean, I heard the story from Amelia and a similar one from Erin, but I didn't put two and two together because there were key details left out. Including mention of a sequined dress."

"It was her high school reunion," I said. "It's not like we went on a date or anything." I didn't know why I was so defensive, but I really hated talking about women with my little sister. And considering that I wasn't sure Erin was even interested in me, or the status of her marriage at this point, I didn't really want to go there.

"Anyway, that dress was for the high school reunion," Zoey began. "With that bastard Nicholas."

Amelia lifted her lip in a snarl, and Tobey raised his brows.

"We don't like Nicholas?" Tobey asked.

"No, we do not," Zoey said with a scowl. "He's an asshole. A cheating asshole who did horrible things. But the divorce is final, and they are no longer together."

"Well, that was quick," I said. I tried to sound casual, but from the looks that all three of them gave me, I knew I hadn't been very proficient at that. Well.

"Yes, she's all single and ready to mingle," Zoey said with a laugh. "Okay, maybe not ready to mingle, but she is single. And I'm going to text you her number so you can see if sparks are indeed flying."

"Don't do that, Zoey," I said quickly.

"What? You don't want her number?" Zoey asked, frowning.

"I didn't say that."

"Yay. Oh, you two will be so cute together," Amelia said, hip-bumping Tobey.

Tobey just gave me a sad smile. "I think you're going to lose in this," he said quietly. "There's two of them against you."

"I thought you would be on my side. That way, we would be two against two." I mock glared, and Tobey just shook his head.

"I can't really win against Amelia. Ever. We know this. We've been friends since we were little. She always wins."

"I really do," Amelia said with a very smug smile.

"Zoey, you shouldn't meddle." I tried to sound stern, but I couldn't help but want the number. I really wanted it. Erin was single? Well, that changed everything. Didn't it?

"I'm just saying, she's already slept over at your house. What's a few conversations by text? Or dare I say maybe even a phone call?" Zoey put her hand on her chest over her heart, and Amelia mock-gasped.

"A phone call? I mean, that's next-level communication." Amelia just grinned as she spoke.

I sighed. "I can't with you. Either of you. I should go anyway. I need to clean up before I head to Greg and Laney's."

"Invite Erin," Zoey said quickly. I froze.

"You want me to invite Erin to my friend's birthday party?"

"Yes. She doesn't have any plans tonight. I checked. And even though it would be weird to ask her any other time for a date the same night, this is different. You could always word it so it's almost like work. You know, like her wanting to check on the cake or something."

"Oh, yes, make it all chemistry-like but add in the work so she doesn't feel overwhelmed." Amelia and Zoey began talking about ways for me to ask Erin out, and I quit listening. I just looked at Tobey and shook my head.

"How does this happen?" I asked. "Please, Tobey. Tell me how this happens."

"One of them is a force to be reckoned with. Two of them? It's the end of all your control. All of your power...gone."

Both women punched him in the arm, and he winced, laughing. "Hey," Tobey growled out.

"Hey, what?" Amelia asked, going nose-to-nose with him. Tobey just grinned and kissed her forehead before pulling back. "Nothing. You always win."

"Yes, I do." Amelia's words were a little whispery, and I couldn't help but notice the blush on her cheeks. I met Zoey's gaze, and we both looked away. I really did not want any part of that. So, I helped my sister for a little bit more, mostly because I didn't want her to have to lift everything on her own. Tobey and I took care of that. And then I headed home. Erin's number in my phone.

I should have gotten it the night she stayed over, but I hadn't. There hadn't been any reason to. Because she had been married at the time. It didn't matter that she had been breaking because of it. She had been married. And that was too much of a complication for me. I didn't want any part of that, especially not with how my parents' marriage had blown up the way it had.

I looked down at my phone and wondered...

Before I could stop myself, I did the craziest thing I could. I called. I didn't text. I called.

Like it was 1999, and I was using a cordless phone instead of a cell. I called.

"Hello?"

"Hey, Erin, it's Devin. Zoey gave me your number. But you don't have to keep talking to me if you don't want to."

"Oh. She said that she might do that as a joke, but I didn't think she actually would." Erin let out a soft, little laugh. The sound went straight to my balls.

Well, fuck.

"Is it okay that I called?"

"Yeah, it's nice. I just...is the cake okay?"

I let out a soft laugh. Zoey and Amelia had been right. Talking about work was helpful.

"The cake is fine. I dropped it off. I'm heading out to the party in a couple hours." I cleared my throat. "Actually, I was wondering if you wanted to go with me."

There was silence. So much silence, I was afraid that I had made a mistake. I was really damn good at making them when it came to women—or anything for that matter.

"To check on the cake?" Erin asked, her voice a little high.

I could have lied. I could have said that it was just about the cake, about wanting her to check on her work. But I didn't want to do that. It sounded like she'd been lied to enough. And I didn't want to be that man.

"No, but you could while we're there. I just thought maybe you'd like to come with me. I know it's short notice, and you probably have things to do. You don't have to say yes. But if you want, I'd love to take you."

"Did Zoey put you up to this?" she asked quietly.

"She mentioned it. I'm not going to lie. I don't want to do that."

"I'm glad you don't want to. Because that would be a deal-breaker for me. Okay? No lies."

"I can do that for you. I'll be honest. So now I'm going to be really honest and say that I thought you looked hot in that dress that night. And really hot today with that flour on your cheek. And I wanted to ask you out, I just didn't know if you were still married or not. So, now that I know that you're not, if you're ready to go out with someone, I hope it'll be me. Tonight. If that's what you want."

I shut my mouth, knowing if I kept going, I'd probably talk myself right out of a date.

"I think that would be fun. And nothing too scary. Just a nice birthday party with friends. That you've known forever. Okay, maybe this is a little scary."

I laughed, shaking my head even though she couldn't see me. "Greg and Laney will be good. And there'll be tons of people that I don't know, so it won't be too much. It's not like my entire family will be there or anything. Plus, you already know some of them."

"I do. And you know my family."

"I do." I paused. "Is that going to be too much for you?"

"No, I don't think so. We're not the people we used to

be. I'm seriously not the person I used to be," she said with a harsh laugh.

"Erin—" I began, but she cut me off.

"Let's do it. Just...will you tell me what time and what I should wear?"

The sense of relief flooding through me was a surprise, but I let out a breath and smiled.

I was going on a date with Erin. The person I told myself I shouldn't pursue when I last saw her.

This was a good step. I couldn't wait to see what would happen tonight.

FIVE

ERIN

———

I STARED AT MY REFLECTION IN THE MIRROR AND wondered if I remembered how to do this. I mean, there had to be a conscious memory or something of how this was done.

I swallowed hard and shook my head. No, I was pretty sure I would never actually remember. Because I hadn't been on a first date since I was what? Fourteen? Or maybe even ten if I really put my mind to it. I had been with Nicholas for so long, the idea of dating made me want to throw up. Not because I still loved him. No, I didn't think that was the case. It was hard to love something that wasn't actually there to begin with.

Somehow, Nicholas had fallen out of love with me. Had started to resent me so much that I was no longer the person he wanted to be with. It was hard to find that love deep inside when there was nothing to claw onto.

No, I didn't love Nicholas anymore. I was just learning how to love myself, frankly.

But I wasn't going to think about that. Because this was not about Nicholas. This was about me. And Devin. And the fact that I was going on a date.

Maybe a bit of an unconventional date. Because Devin had asked me out that afternoon, and here I was, getting ready tonight. For a group date. At a party for one of his friends. An event where I could say I was just checking up on the cake, on my work, rather than actually going on a date with Devin.

But even though he had given me that excuse, that's all it was. An excuse.

I was going on a first date with Devin Carr, and I had butterflies.

That flutter in the stomach that said that this was something new and exciting and different. It was thrilling and scary and made me want to throw up and yet dance at the same time.

Well, maybe not exactly at the same time.

Wasn't that just a picture?

I pulled my blond hair back from my face. I wondered if I should just wear it up and then let it fall down in its odd waves that did their own thing if I didn't straighten the strands.

I hadn't wanted to wash it again since I had just done it that morning, so that meant dry shampoo, maybe a curl or two, and a prayer.

I really wasn't good at this dating thing. I think I was an actual virgin at it.

That made me snort. I'd been married to Nicholas for far too long, and with him for even longer. There was nothing virginal about me. Other than the fact that I had only slept with one guy in my life.

I let my hair fall and put my hands under my face.

Was I going to sleep with Devin tonight? No, it wasn't even a real date. It was almost a work outing. Okay, it wasn't that. But there would be tons of his friends, people I didn't know, all celebrating the fortieth birthday of a man I had made a cake for.

There was no way that I was going to sleep with Devin Carr after that.

Unless I wanted to.

Unless *he* wanted to.

Did he want to?

I shook my head and let my hands fall from my face, then moved them around to my temples.

I rubbed and tried to work out the worry, the brewing

headache. Only I was a very good worrier and, sometimes, there was no working it out.

I was losing my mind, and all because I had said yes to a *maybe* date. And because Devin had given me no time to formulate a good excuse for why I might be busy. Because, you know, I might actually have a life.

I couldn't back out.

Why did I feel like I was doing everything wrong?

I sighed and then went to pull on some white jeans, forgetting at the last moment that I wanted to change my underwear, too. Not for Devin. This was *not* for Devin. No, it was because I was wearing white jeans and I wasn't about to wear my work panties, the nice, wide ones that were not for public consumption but totally covered everything as I moved around my kitchen.

Plus, I had been wearing black that day. So that really wouldn't work.

I quickly switched to a white, lacy thong, and not because Devin would see. No, this was because of the jeans. And I liked these jeans.

I was probably going to stay in these jeans all night and stain them because that's what I did. I was bound to do something that ruined them, but that was fine.

Everything was fine.

I slid on the pants, put on a black bandeau, and then pulled on my shirt. It was an off-the-shoulder black top that had bell sleeves and billowed out just enough after it tapered in to the waist. That way, it covered what I needed it to cover, and I still felt pretty.

I put on black sandals with a wedge, the silver adornments on the top the perfect complement to the jewelry I planned on wearing.

I didn't really know what kind of dress code the party had for the night, but considering the cake I had made, and Devin telling me to wear anything I wanted, I figured it wasn't formal. So, I wasn't willing to wear a dress. After all, this wasn't a real date. And even if the night went poorly, it wouldn't matter. Because it wasn't like this would become anything serious.

I already had serious. I'd had years of serious.

This could just be a fling.

Yes, I told myself. A fling. But I wasn't even going to have sex with Devin. He was just going to be my friend.

But if it turned into a fling, that was fine. Though I was never going down the road of a relationship again. Been there, got the T-shirt. And then saw the T-shirt stripped off the damn cheerleader as my husband fucked her and did drugs off her chest.

I growled and slid on my hoop earrings, trying to slow down my breathing.

I didn't know if Nicholas was still doing coke or if that had just been a one-time thing.

I hadn't asked. Didn't want anything to do with it.

I got my half of our old life and walked away.

It hurt to think that he might be hurting himself, but there was nothing I could do about it. He had walked away first.

And I didn't want to fight it anymore.

No, I was not going to think about that. I couldn't. Tonight was all about the date. The not-date. The I-have-no-idea-what-I'm-doing date.

See? Everything was fine. I didn't have to think about what was going to happen tonight.

I just had to be. Something I was getting better at. After all, I'd had six months to figure out who I was. Tonight was just the next step in that.

My phone buzzed on my dresser, and I looked down at it, my heart in my throat.

Was it Devin wanting to cancel? I wouldn't be surprised. After all, this had been short notice. Maybe he had decided that taking me to his friend's birthday party was too much. After all, wasn't it a statement?

My hands shook, and I cursed at myself, annoyed that I was always nervous when it came to Devin—or anyone at this point.

But then I relaxed, seeing my sister's name on the screen.

I picked up the cell, still staring at myself in the mirror like a weirdo. "Hey, Jenn, what's up?" I asked, smiling.

I loved my sister. She'd always been there for me, even when our parents weren't. After all, our dad walking out on us because he just didn't want a family or whatever story he'd told our mother kind of changed things when we were growing up.

Our mom was a little insane. Okay, a lot. Probably clinically, but she refused to get help. She left us as soon as I turned eighteen, and then it was just Jenn and me. And Jenn's family. I loved Jenn's family.

"Hey there, Jitterbug," Jenn said, and I laughed.

"Jitterbug?" I asked.

"What? I'm trying out new things. Junebug. Jitterbug. I don't know. I'll think of something."

"We live in Colorado. Not Texas."

"Colorado is getting a twang, haven't you heard? It's all the Texans moving up here."

"Are we going to start saying 'dude' more often since we're also being filled up by Californians?" I asked, smiling again.

"I don't know about y'all, dude, but sometimes my accent has no idea what it's doing." She added a heavy drawl and a surfer dialect all at the same time, and I couldn't help but laugh.

"I love you."

"I love you, too, darlin'." She drawled out the word *darlin'* like she was a cowgirl, and I just snorted.

"What's up, Jenn?"

"I was just checking in on you since I haven't heard from you in a couple of days." My sister pulled the phone away as she yelled at one of her children in a nice, happy tone, but it was a mom yell, nonetheless. I could just picture the look on her face. Jenn was an amazing mother. And her husband was one incredible dad.

And though our mom had tried her best, it hadn't been the best. It had been adequate. We'd had a roof over our heads and food in our mouths, but not much more. It wasn't what Jenn gave her daughters.

But our mom had worked long hours, and after a while, I was pretty sure she resented us. Now, she was off in a commune of all places, learning to be one with the world and putting herself first for the first time in her life.

And while I applauded her for putting herself first because, hell, all moms should do that sometimes, she had cut ties with us in the process. And I was pretty sure she hadn't met a single grandchild.

That wasn't something I could forgive. Not for my sake, it didn't affect me, but for Jenn's.

"I'm fine," I said after Jenn got back on the line.

"Oh, you keep saying that, but I worry about you. You are my little sister."

"I'm fine. Just working."

"That douchebag hasn't come by and bothered you?" Jenn asked, a sharp sting to her tone.

Jenn had never been a fan of Nicholas. Oh, they'd gotten along just fine at holidays and things, but she'd always wanted me to ditch my boyfriend from high school and find someone else. To live life a little before I settled down with a man that had been my one and only. Well, just because my sister ended up being right about that didn't mean I wanted to think about it. Damn it.

"He hasn't bothered me at all."

"His stuff's still in your garage?"

"Yeah, but it's not a big deal. I'm fine. Really."

"You say that, but until I see you happy and settled again, I'm not going to believe you."

I pinched the bridge of my nose. We'd always had this problem. We had issues. We were siblings. We had been born to fight, even as we loved each other.

"I'm never going to get married again. I did that already. And you're doing wonderful at that. I'm just going to be the cool aunt Erin."

"You already are the cool aunt Erin. You were the cool aunt Erin when you had that douchebag, Nicholas."

"Do your kids know you call him 'douchebag?'"

"They're in the other room with Steve. Everything's fine."

"I love you."

"I love you, too," she said.

"But you need to get some dick."

I snorted and looked at myself in the mirror again. "Stop it." I sobered, remembering the last conversation we'd had, and why it had been a couple of days since we talked.

"We need to talk about Dad," I said softly.

"No, we really don't. I'm done with him. He walked

away. Just because you got a stick up your butt where you actually feel like you need to figure out what our dear old dad's doing right now, doesn't mean I have to deal with it."

"All I'm saying is that we know nothing about him. And I'd like to know."

"I don't know why you do. He was an asshole. Is an asshole. He left us high and dry. He left, and Mom broke. That's partly why she is the way she is. That's why she hasn't seen my babies. The two of them can fuck right off. You and me? We're the only family we need. I am done with him. You get me?"

There was such brittleness to my sister's tone. Pain. I knew she had to be done. Just because I wanted to find and figure out the man who had helped to give us life, didn't mean that Jenn needed to. Though I still wanted her to be a part of my plan.

I'd gotten the idea to find out where he was after I finished signing my divorce paperwork. It was as if casting off one part of my life while trying to look forward made me want to look at the pieces I'd hidden so long ago.

I didn't even remember my dad's face. Oh, I could look at photos, but I didn't recall him smiling down at me. I didn't remember him lifting me up and setting me on his shoulders. I didn't even know if he had ever done that.

I didn't know any of it.

I hated him for leaving.

And I hated myself for wanting more.

"Just be okay with what you have," Jenn said, her voice soothing.

"You say that, but you said I needed to get dick," I said, quickly changing the subject.

She barked out a laugh. "You do need to get dick."

"Then how can I be fine with myself if I need dick."

"Oh, stop it. I'm saying, don't look behind you, just look forward. Okay?"

"Okay."

The doorbell rang, and I cursed.

"Who is that?" she asked.

"My date."

She started speaking a mile a minute, and I tried to stop her. "It's fine. Just a date."

"Well, it's about time. You need penis. All the dick. Go, you!"

"I love you, ya dirty whore," I said, laughing.

"I love you, too, filthy slut."

I hung up, shaking my head as I went down to the front door.

Yes, my sister and I had issues, and we fought, but we loved each other. Even if we were weird.

I took a deep breath, then I opened the door, my eyes widening.

"Damn. You know I liked the glittery dress, but I think I like you in those jeans even more."

I grinned at Devin's words and tried to swallow hard. It

wasn't really working out too well. I could barely catch my breath.

I knew Devin was hot. Hello, everyone knew he was hot. I'd been pressed up against him before in my life, but it had been more me feeling out of it after drinking a little too much after my world shattered. But the way he looked now? I couldn't even get my thoughts together. His jeans were molded to his thighs, tight, a little worn at the seams but the perfect fit. He had on dark boots that matched his dark belt. He had on a collared shirt, one that buttoned up, but he'd only tucked in the front, he hadn't finished tucking in the back. It might have looked sloppy on someone else, but somehow, he made it work. He looked sexy as fuck.

I knew I was in trouble. I'd known I was screwed the moment he walked into my bakery. And then when he texted me and called.

I knew I was in trouble.

But I didn't think I cared.

Not right then.

Not when I couldn't keep my eyes off the muscles in his forearms, or fail to notice the way his jaw ticked just slightly when he stared at me.

I couldn't focus when I watched the long line of his neck as he swallowed, or the way his eyes narrowed when he studied me.

I couldn't focus. All I could do was watch his hands and

notice how wide his palms were, how strong and thick his fingers were.

And how I couldn't help but think about that story I had heard about the length of a man's dick in conjunction with the size of his feet or his hands.

I refused to look down at his jeans.

I wouldn't look down at his feet.

I was a goner.

And I was really worried that I was going to fuck this up.

"You don't look too bad yourself," I said quickly, smiling.

"Thanks for that. But, seriously, you look sexy as hell. And I promise I won't say that again if it makes you blush and look as nervous as you do right now."

I put my hands up to my cheeks and cocked my head. "Sorry. I'm not good at this."

"I think you're doing just fine."

He smiled then, and I let out a shaky breath as I reached for my purse and gift and then followed him out to his truck.

"Your truck is just as amazing as I remember it."

"I'm glad you remember it at all from that night."

I shoved at his shoulder, even though he didn't move an inch.

The man was strong, steady, and the ink that covered him? I seriously wanted to follow the lines with my tongue.

See? I was losing my damn mind.

"I wasn't that drunk."

"Still slept on my couch."

I knew I was blushing again.

"Let's just forget about that, shall we? Like, let's not talk about it at all."

"I don't know if I can actually agree to that." He helped me into the truck, then went around to his side. As he got in, I frowned.

"Why can't you agree to that?"

"If I do, how am I going to remember the first time you slept over?"

"Smooth moves."

"I try."

We talked about work, mostly his with a little bit of mine. It was nice. It didn't feel like a first date, maybe because it wasn't a date. But it didn't really feel like a first of anything. After all, I had slept at his house already. And I knew him. Even if it was on the periphery.

Devin wasn't a complete stranger. I just had to keep reminding myself of that.

"We're here," he said, pulling up in front of a house. There were a few cars there, and I looked around, smiling at the neighborhood. "You know, I almost bought a house in this neighborhood."

"Really? It's a good place. I live two neighborhoods over."

"I remember," I said, meeting his gaze.

"I thought you didn't want to talk about that night."

"Apparently, I'm not very good at that."

"I don't mind."

He helped me out of the truck, and then pulled out a bottle of wine in a little bag as well as a gift bag from the back seat.

I tugged the card and little gift bag out of my small purse and looked up at him.

"So, I didn't really know what to get him as a gift, so I got him a little knick-knack for his desk. It's stupid. But I was kind of out of ideas."

"You didn't need to get him anything. I got him something." He shook the bag. "Plus, I brought wine. I figured you could bring that."

"That would have been smart."

"Hey, I gave you like thirty minutes' notice. I think it'd have been okay if you didn't bring a gift."

"Well, we'll see. This is pretty much nothing."

"So you say."

He held out his hand, and I slid my fingers into his, ignoring the way my breath caught.

His hands were working-man's hands. Considering that he lifted boxes and dealt with letters and God only knew what else every day, I assumed that's where he got the calluses.

But when he slid the pad of his thumb across my hand, I swallowed hard.

I couldn't help but picture those hands in other places.

Maybe everyone else was right. Perhaps I did need dick. Because if I was thinking about him like this with just the two of us holding hands? I was in a whole load of trouble.

Greg and Laney were amazing. They not only loved their cake to the point where Greg had picked me up and twirled me around like I was a marionette doll, but they also had incredible food, good beer, and just threw a great party.

They'd built a whole back deck and patio onto their home that had two different floors to it.

They hadn't put in a pool, but there was a hot tub with a couple of brave people getting in just for kicks and giggles.

I stayed with Devin most of the night since I didn't really know anybody, and the whole idea that I'd come to check on the cake would clearly be a ruse that nobody would believe.

Everybody knew that I was on a date with the elusive Devin Carr, and they wanted to know who I was, who my people were, and how I had met him.

When people found out that I was the little sister of a girl he used to date? That had been fun.

"Oh, going through the family, are we?" one man asked, and Devin just growled.

"Watch your mouth," he said.

"Oh, I am. Just think it's interesting, that's all."

"Seriously? It's been how many years?"

"I know, right?" he asked. He paused, and I looked up at him. "It's not a problem for me. Is it a problem for you?" he asked.

I shook my head, setting down my empty glass. "No. If you were still pining for her, or if she was pining for *you* at all, maybe it would be an issue. But it's not."

"Okay, then," he said. He squeezed my hand, and the two of us walked around a bit to say goodbye before heading out.

Now, we were standing on my porch, having left the party a little early.

"About Jenn..." I said out of the blue, still thinking about my sister.

"You think she's pining for me?" Devin asked, laughter in his eyes.

"I don't think so. I mentioned to her that I was going on a date tonight," I began.

"Oh?"

"I didn't mention you, though."

"Is there a reason for that?"

"No. I just didn't have time. I mentioned it right when you rang the doorbell," I added.

"Ah. But it's not a problem for me."

"Okay," I whispered.

"What was that voice for?"

"It's not a problem that you used to date her. But I want

you to know, I'm not ready for a big relationship. I just got out of a huge one."

"Okay," he said, sliding his hands into his pockets.

"So, you're not worried about the fact that I used to date your sister. A whole hell of a long time ago."

"I'm not worried about that. I just don't know exactly what I want."

He took a few steps forward. When he reached his hand up to my face, I didn't flinch, didn't pull away. When he trailed his fingers along my cheekbone, I sucked in a breath. My skin pebbled, and my breath hitched before slowly sliding out again.

"I don't think it needs to be serious on day one," Devin whispered. "But that's up to you."

I swallowed hard, trying to get my thoughts in order. It was always hard around him. And by always, I meant the three times I had seen him since we became adults.

I didn't know what to say. Didn't know if there was anything to say at all.

Instead, I just looked up at him and then parted my lips, wanting to say something.

But there was nothing to say. Then, suddenly, his lips were on mine, and I couldn't think at all.

Six

Devin

I COULDN'T THINK, COULDN'T BREATHE, COULDN'T do anything. I knew I needed to pull back, needed to get my tongue out of her mouth, and not let my beard scrape her jaw, but I couldn't. I couldn't do anything.

I knew we were on her damn porch, both of us out in the open where anyone could see, and all I could do was want her, need her, and taste her.

Damn, she tasted like Heaven. Like that margarita she'd sipped at all night mixed with a sweet and spicy taste that was all Erin.

Fucking. Erin.

Yeah, that's what I wanted to do. I wanted to push her against the door, pull down those tight jeans, and fuck her hard until we were both sweaty, sated, and panting.

And from the feel of my dick pressing into my zipper, I had a feeling that just might happen if I didn't pull away right then.

So, I did the one thing that might kill me and my cock—I pulled away.

I rested my forehead on hers, both of our breaths coming out a bit choppily.

"We're on your front steps. Anyone can walk by." I sucked in a breath, trying to calm my heart. But it was hard when she was pressed against me. The hard line of my cock pushed against my jeans as I swore to myself. I tried to move closer to her. No, that was all my hips. But I couldn't help it. She was just so damn sexy. So freaking hot. And she was in my arms.

"Oh," she said, her eyes wide, the look in them a little wild.

"Do you want me to leave? I can leave right now. We can stop."

She looked at me then, her hand sliding down my chest, her nails raking just a bit. I couldn't really feel it through my shirt, but if I'd been naked? It would have hurt in the best kind of way. Damn it, I really needed to stop thinking about

Erin like this. But I couldn't help it. She was right here in my arms. And she wanted me. I wanted her.

Maybe...maybe it could work.

"Why don't we go inside?" she breathed. I nodded. Then, somehow, we were both inside, my mouth on hers again, and her back pressed against the door. I didn't remember closing it, didn't remember sliding my hands around her hips then under her ass to lift her up. She was pressed against the door, her legs wrapped around my waist as I rotated my hips ever so slightly, rubbing my jean-clad cock against her.

She moaned, nipping at my chin, then my lips. Then we were kissing again, her hands sliding through my hair and then down my neck, her nails scraping just a little against my skin. I shivered and nibbled on her jaw, then licked her neck and bit down on her shoulder.

She was the one to shiver this time, and I grinned. Then I kissed her again.

"I want to be inside you," I growled.

"Then why aren't you inside of me already?"

I grinned and then nipped at her lips again. "I want to take it slow with you."

"Slow?" She cocked her head to the side. "Why slow?"

"Because maybe you need slow."

"Maybe I don't." She slid her hands between us and squeezed my cock through my jeans.

My eyes crossed, and I swore I saw stars. Jesus Christ, she was hot.

And, yeah, she had only been with one person, that much I had gathered. That damn Nicholas. Her ex-husband, the one who had cheated on her.

What if I wasn't good enough for her? What if I went too fast, and she realized that all sex was a bust?

Great, no pressure.

Erin squeezed my dick again, and I swallowed hard. "You do that again, it's going to be over mighty quickly. Even before I get inside you."

"Then stop thinking so hard."

I traced my finger along her cheekbone, needing to calm myself for just a moment.

"What if we need to think just a bit more? Not hard, just a bit."

Her face shuttered for just a moment, and then she gave me a tight nod. I knew I'd said the wrong thing, but...fuck. I didn't want to hurt her. She'd been hurt enough.

"I'm sorry if this is too much—"

I cut her off. "Stop it. I have my hands on you, and I really want to be inside you right now. This isn't too much. I just don't want to go too fast and miss out on you. I want to touch every part of you. Learn every taste. I want to know every inch of you with my tongue. And I want to fuck you hard and slow until you come. And I want you to come more than once. And for you to do that, we need to go a little bit slower. Because you keep squeezing my dick like you are? I'm not going to last, babe. I'm not a young kid anymore."

"There's nothing old about you, damn it."

I grinned. "Maybe. But I'm going to blow my load right in my jeans like a teenager if you don't stop."

"So, you're saying you're too young *and* too old right now?" she asked, her eyes dancing with laughter. Good, she should be laughing, not worried about what she had been thinking about before. Because I didn't want to see that shuttered look on her face again. I didn't want to be the person who brought her there.

"What if we do a little bit of everything?" she asked, her voice a little breathy.

"Oh?"

"What if we do exactly what we need, and then go a little slower later? I mean, that is if you can handle more than once."

My dick stood at attention, and I narrowed my eyes. "That sounds like a challenge."

"No. You're the one pressing me up against this door. I'm just saying."

"Okay, then. You asked for it."

"Yeah, I did." I growled and kissed her again.

I swept my hands through her hair, tightening my grip just

enough. She tilted her neck to the side, and I latched on, nipping and biting and sucking. I felt like a damn vampire, but I loved the taste of her skin. I wanted more. So I trailed my fingers along her collarbone, tugging her sleeves down. She didn't have anything on her shoulders, and that was just so damn sexy. It gave me access to all that skin to bite and lick and watch.

Damn, I loved her taste.

She tugged her arms out of her sleeves, and I pulled at the bottom of her shirt so it popped over her breasts.

She wore a strapless thing that I pulled down to reveal a lace, strapless bra, her nipples halfway out of the cups.

"Dear God," I growled.

"Yeah, not the best bra. I think I'm a little too big for it."

"No, don't. I'm going to need a minute."

"Another minute?"

"Jesus Christ. I knew I loved your breasts from just what I'd seen in that dress and around. But in this bra? It's like it's a feast. Yep, those nipples are calling to me. Look, they're saying my name."

"You are such a dork."

"Pretty much." I lowered my head and sucked one nipple into my mouth, letting it go with a pop.

She shivered in my hold, and I bit down before moving to her other breast, tugging the lace down so I could access the rest of her.

She was more than a handful, but not two. It was the perfect amount for me. And I had really big-ass hands.

I slowly molded her breast in my hand, using my hips to keep her pressed against the door. It probably wasn't the most comfortable position, but I couldn't help it. I just needed her this way.

I used the callused part of my thumbs to scrape across her nipples, and she arched her back, pressing her breasts more firmly into the palms of my hands.

I squeezed and molded and lowered my head to suck and lick. She squirmed, her core hot against my jeans-clad dick.

I knew if we weren't careful, we'd both end up on the floor and not in a comfortable way, so I let go but held onto her hips.

"Hey, I was almost finished," she whispered.

"That's good. But I don't want us to get concussions from falling to the damn floor."

"Oh. That's probably a good idea."

I carried her a few steps into the living room, then sat her down on the edge of the couch and went to town on her breasts again. I couldn't help it. Her tits were magnificent.

I sucked, molded, and bit down, leaving kisses on the skin between her breasts before moving down to her belly. She wiggled as I knelt down, slowly undoing her pants.

Thankfully, she helped me lift up her ass as I slid off her jeans. I growled when I looked at her.

"Matching panties?"

"Just a thong because it worked with the jeans. I didn't really think you'd be seeing it."

Interesting. When she blushed, she flushed all fucking over.

Now that was fucking amazing.

I spread her legs on the edge of the couch and just looked at her, wanting her.

I pushed a little farther back, my hands on her knees, and she blushed even more.

"Devin."

"What? I just want to look."

"But you're not touching. Not really."

"You want me to touch?" I asked, tilting my head.

"I need you to."

"Right answer."

I slid one hand up her thigh and slowly rubbed my thumb along her mound over her panties. She sucked in a breath, her hands digging into the side of the couch. I kept one hand firmly on her other thigh so she wouldn't fall back and paid special attention. I pinched her panties together so the material tightened just over her clit, and then slowly tugged them up and down, playing with her clit and her outer folds.

She panted, wiggling on the couch. I leaned forward and blew and breathed cool and then warm air on her.

"Devin."

"I'm not done yet."

I leaned forward and licked her in one long swipe that sent us both into moans.

"You taste like Heaven."

"I...I need more."

"I'll give you more." And then I did. I slid her panties to the side, threw both thighs over my shoulders, and then I ate.

And licked. And sucked. Spread her with my fingers as I went deeper. When I speared her with two digits, she shouted my name and came, tightening so hard around my fingers, I was afraid she might break me. Damn, I couldn't wait to get my cock inside of her.

I let her adjust to me as she came down from her orgasm and then slid my fingers in and out of her, using my thumb to play with her clit as I leaned forward to bite and lick at her.

She wiggled more on the couch, trying to pull away, but I kept going.

"Devin, it's too much."

"We've only just begun."

And so I made her come again. When she did, she leaned back, almost falling off the couch. I quickly slid my fingers out of her, leaned up to kiss her hard on the mouth, and then used the wetness on my fingers to trace her lips.

"Taste yourself," I ordered.

Her tongue dashed out, and her eyes widened as she licked at my fingers.

"Good girl."

I kissed her again, tasting her on my tongue, my lips, just everywhere.

And because her body was shaking against me, I pulled her forward to a stand so she was leaning against the back of the couch with me in front of her.

"That was kind of ..." she whispered. I just grinned.

"At a loss for words?"

"I think so."

"Good."

"What about you?"

"We're not done yet, baby."

"Oh."

She went to her knees immediately, trying to undo my belt, and I shook my head, kind of pulling away from her.

"Next time. After I come the first time inside you. I don't think I'm going to last long if your mouth goes around me."

She frowned. "But you went down on me. Don't I need to go down on you, too? I mean it's only fair."

I shook my head, frowning.

I pulled her up again so she was standing in front of me, naked except for her thong pushed off to the side, and just cupped her cheeks, staring down at her. "If you want to, you can. Maybe not right now since I'm so on edge. But I did that to pleasure you. Because it pleased me. You never have to give me a blowjob just because I ate you out. It was exactly what I wanted to do. Do I want those lips around my cock? Fuck, yeah. But it's not a tit for tat thing."

"I thought you liked tits. Or were those tats?"

I threw my head back and laughed. "Okay. You got me there. But it's not a *have to* thing. Okay? No matter what we do between us, it's never a requirement."

I really hoped she got that because I had a feeling that what she'd said hadn't been about me. No, it was about her douche of an ex. And since I didn't want him between us, and I didn't want him anywhere near this room, I pushed him from my thoughts and planned to do my best to push him from hers, as well.

I kissed her again and then pulled back so I could tug my shirt over my head.

"Now, turn over and bend just slightly as you take off that thong."

She raised her brow. "Are we doing porn now?" she asked with a laugh.

"Maybe. But I need time to take off my shoes, so I figured I'd watch your ass work as I do."

"Well, that's a good answer." She turned, went to her toes, and then bent just slightly to pull off her thong.

Yeah, she was going to kill me. Every damn curve. Every touch of skin. I wasn't going to last long. Just looking at that ass of hers. Or her tits. Or her...anything right then just about did me in.

I took off my shoes and my socks and undid my jeans, and then I was naked, standing in front of her in the middle of her living room. I just wanted to fuck her hard right there.

Dear God. It was so hard to stay in control when she was around. It had been easier when I knew she was taken. Easier when I didn't want to think about it. But now? Things were weird. I hadn't meant for this to happen. I hadn't meant for any of this to happen when I walked into the bakery that morning. But here we were, naked in her living room and about to fuck. Hard. But it had to be just fucking. It couldn't be anything more. Right? No, it couldn't be. Neither of us wanted anything else.

Right?

Before I could let those thoughts muddle my brain, she took a step forward and slid her hand around my length. When she squeezed slightly, I groaned.

"You are way too good with those hands."

"I would say the same to you, but I don't want to say, 'way too good' because I think you are just right."

"That's good to hear. Now, I have a condom in my wallet. It's still good, I can promise you that. But I only have the one. I wasn't planning for this." I looked at her then, hoping she could see the sincerity in my statement.

She gave me a nod and then a shy smile. "I don't have any condoms in the house. I wasn't expecting this either."

I didn't know why that made my chest warm like it did. She hadn't been with her ex here. There wasn't anything of him in this house. At least, not physically. That was good. It had to be good.

"Okay, then we better make it count."

I bent over and kind of slid the condom out of my wallet, knowing it wasn't the best place to put it, but a man needed to keep it somewhere. I rolled it over my length, watching her eyes track my movements. I did it slowly. So slow, I was probably torturing myself, too, but I loved the way her pupils dilated, and her hand unconsciously went to her nipple, pinching ever so slightly.

Yeah, she was my dirty girl.

I couldn't wait to slide into her.

"Now, where am I going to fuck you?" I pinched and squeezed the base of my cock, keeping myself steady as I looked around.

"Not the bedroom? she asked.

"No, that's where I'll eat you out after."

"Oh?" She blushed again, all the way down to the tips of those pink breasts.

Perfection.

"Maybe this table?" I walked over and put my weight on it. "Yeah, it's sturdy enough. Come here."

"You do like ordering me around."

I raised a brow. "And?"

"I think I'm okay with that."

When she came over, I grabbed the back of her head, kissing her hard.

I slid one hand to her hip, helping her to the edge of the table. And then I was between her legs, the tip of my erection teasing her folds. She was already so wet, so hot, I knew she was going to be tight. But, damn.

We both froze. Our breaths coming in pants.

"Are you ready?" I asked her. She nodded, looking down between us. "Don't want to go too fast. I don't want to hurt you."

"I don't think you can," she whispered.

I wondered right then if she had told a lie. I didn't think the statement was just about being physical.

I slowly slid inside of her, one terrifyingly slow inch at a time. She sucked in a breath and then cradled my cheek. She was impossibly tight, even after everything we had already done. But that just meant she was even more swollen. I swallowed hard, watching her face as I slid my length into her. Her eyes were wide, her mouth parted, her pupils dilated. She was so sexy. It was hard for me to concentrate. But I would. Because she deserved this. She deserved so much.

When she gripped my arms, I swallowed hard again and then slid in to the hilt. Both of us groaned as I did.

"Devin."

"Yeah. I feel it." She looked at me then, her hands on the

table, my hands on her hips. And then I moved. I worked in and out of her, slowly at first, pulling out inch by inch and then sliding back in just as slowly. It was if we were moving and rocking on a boat, ever so slightly, with a lull between each wave. And then I sped up, moving faster and faster until both of us were panting, and the sounds were wet and hot and needy. She pulled one leg up higher on my hip, and I went deeper, both of us moaning again.

When I shifted one hand from her so I could move it over her clit, my callused thumb sliding over her, she screamed my name, coming again. When she clamped down on my dick, I came, too. Filling her up even though I knew it was in the condom.

I groaned, the base of my spine tingling, and my balls tight as I orgasmed hard.

My legs shook. My knees were weak. She leaned on me, her body limp, and I knew that was possibly the best sex I'd ever had in my life.

And there'd only been a bit of foreplay.

Even as I was inside her, still semi-hard, still wanting more, I knew that this couldn't just be the first and only night. There had to be more.

But I was so afraid she would say no.

She looked up at me then, sliding her hands through my hair as she smiled shyly. She looked timid every once in a while. But I didn't usually think of her that way. She was strong. Had always been so strong.

"That was amazing," she whispered. "I don't know what to say."

I kissed her again, slowly working my tongue in and out of her mouth.

Then I pulled away and pulled out of her. I didn't want to make a mistake with the condom, so that meant not staying inside her for as long as I wanted to.

"I'd better clean us up. But that was amazing, so fucking perfect."

She blushed, and I helped her off the table.

I walked her towards the bedroom, thankfully easy to find since the layout of the house made sense. We moved to her bathroom, and I used a washcloth and warm water to clean her up and then myself after I had disposed of the condom.

It was a little awkward, knowing that our clothes were in the living room and both of us were naked in her bathroom, but I didn't want to go back out there and get dressed just yet. It would feel a bit cold, slightly clinical.

"I don't know if I cuddle afterwards," she said, laughing. "And that's a weird thing to say."

"No, I was about to ask you if you liked to. I was going to carry you to the bed and do just that, but I didn't want it to be too much for you on the first night."

She nodded, sobering just a little. And it gave me a clutch in my belly. Fuck, would this be the brush off?

"I don't want to hurt you. I don't want to use you in

any way. I don't normally do this. Or ever. I've never done this."

"I know."

Fuck.

"But I'm not looking for anything serious. I can't. I've never *not* had serious. Does that make sense? Does that make me out to be like a slut or something?"

I growled and cupped her face. "Get that thought right out of your head. Even if this is the one and only night we ever do this, you're not a fucking slut. You made a conscious decision, and we had very amazing sex. If this is all you want, that's fine."

Lie. Once wasn't fine. But I wasn't going to make her feel bad about herself either.

"Do you get me?"

She nodded. "I get you. It was just a stupid thought."

"Not stupid. But fine. Just don't have it again."

"You can't tell me what to think, Devin."

"I can do my best. But...you don't want serious? Okay. We can try that. 'Cause I want to be your friend, Erin." I didn't really realize the truth of that statement until I had said the words out loud. But there they were. And I couldn't take them back.

"Like friends with benefits?" she asked, that same shy look from before on her face.

"Well, yeah. We can make that work. Right?"

"Right."

And even though she'd said the words, I had a feeling neither of us knew exactly what that meant.

But I didn't want to say goodbye to her. Not fully. Not when I didn't really know what was going on. I didn't know what I wanted. And I had a feeling she didn't really know either.

But what we'd had tonight? It meant something. I had a feeling we would have to figure out what that was.

SEVEN

ERIN

———

MY LIPS WERE STILL SWOLLEN, I HAD BEARD BURN
on my inner thighs, and I was sore in all the right places. Yet
I couldn't really be too excited about it or think about it at
all because I was waiting for Nicholas to show up.

How was this my life?

I legit didn't know anymore.

I hadn't seen my ex-husband since he left. Vacated the
home we'd shared for years. He'd walked out of the house
that day, but he'd walked out of my life long before that.
Honestly, a little earlier than I'd even thought.

Because if he'd actually been with me this past year, maybe we'd have made it. Perhaps he'd have loved me.

Maybe I would still love him.

I rubbed the skin over my heart with my fist and let out a long sigh.

My thoughts felt like they were going in a thousand different directions. It was a little hard to think about the fact that I'd just been with Devin last night, and now this. I couldn't process it. How was I supposed to sort through it all?

I didn't remember what I had said to my friends after I slept with Nicholas the first time. I could only remember that it hadn't lasted that long, and it had hurt—and not in a good way. But we had gotten better at it over time. Nicholas had been my only until now. My first. And until I walked in on him banging an ex-high school cheerleader, I had thought that he would be my one and only. My last. I had been so wrong. So wrong. But when it came to him, it seemed I had been wrong about a lot of things.

I didn't like myself when I thought about him. I didn't like that I felt like I was getting bitter, feeling a little more like I wanted to talk bad about him and just live in my angst and anger.

So, when I told him that I wanted a divorce, I had tried to push him out of my mind.

I had grieved the loss of our relationship. I had mourned

for the person I no longer was. Honestly, I had even been sad about the years we lost.

But I didn't know if I could really be at the point where I could say "well, at least we had those years. At least I had time to change and become the person I am."

Because I currently stewed in my anger about Nicholas. I was steeped in a feeling of being lost and the fact that I didn't know who I was anymore. So, I wasn't sure I could say that I cherished the time we had together. It was as if a cloud of darkness had been painted over them, and I couldn't quite comprehend exactly what had been good or bad.

There must have been some decent years. I didn't like to think I was the type of person who would have stayed no matter how hard the bad spots got. Or when and if those bad spots became terrible. What I did know is that I couldn't just push through the bad parts anymore. I didn't know what that said about me. And because I didn't know, I tried to push it all away and become a different person once the divorce was finalized.

But I wasn't really sure what would happen next. With me. With Devin. Or with my ex-husband, who would be at my front door any minute.

I looked down at my hands and fisted them in front of me.

I had cried, and I had come home.

Cried.

Not from shame. But something *was* different inside of me. What we'd shared had been the best sex of my life. Perhaps one of the best moments of my life period.

And it had been shared with a man who wasn't my husband.

I had thought that Nicholas would be my forever, my happily ever after and all of that where you go riding off into the sunset with the love of your life. But that wasn't meant to be. And now I had slept with another man. It had been different. And warm. And amazing. I had been brazen and loved it. I'd asked for exactly what I wanted and got it and more. Devin had been careful, caring, both hard and fast, exactly what I needed. Actually, he'd been exactly what I hadn't known I needed.

But when I got home, it had been too much. I'd showered, washing him off, not because I didn't want him to stay, but because I needed to find myself again.

What was wrong with me? Why did I have this need to constantly discover who I was when it didn't make any sense at all?

I was still sore because it had been long enough at this point since I had been with any man, and Devin was different.

A good kind of different.

I didn't know what that meant. Especially because I didn't want another relationship. I had been honest with Devin, and I hoped he had been truthful with me. Because I had been there. Done that. I didn't want to get married again. I didn't want to rely on someone to the point where I could have my heart broken again. I wanted to find out who this new me was. Because I loved my job, and I enjoyed parts of my life. I just wanted to fix the rest of it. But I didn't need a man to do that.

So, I would find this new Erin. The new woman who happened to sleep with Devin Carr.

And I would have fun, I would be respectful, and I would be respected at the same time. Because Devin would take care of me. And I would do my damndest to take care of him.

As long as neither of us had to truly rely on each other.

Maybe thinking that made me a bad person. But then again, I would find out exactly what kind of person I was, wouldn't I?

I needed to put Devin out of my thoughts for now, though, because I didn't want to think about him while Nicholas was in my territory.

I growled under my breath.

My ex had called that morning, waking me up after a nice sleep-in. I had the whole day off, something I tried to give myself once a week even if I didn't always make it happen. And though I was still working online on things and planning things out, I wasn't in the bakery. My staff was handling that part for me. It wasn't easy handing over the reins, and I didn't do it often, but today was supposed to be that day. So, of course, Nicholas just had to ruin it for me.

He always ruined things.

"No, I'm not going to think like that. I'm not going to let him wreck this for me."

I growled just a little at myself and rolled back my shoulders as I paced my living room. When we split up our belongings and sold the house, Nicholas had moved into a small condo, not knowing what his next step was. That meant that all the junk he'd kept in the garage didn't fit at his new place. And, for some reason, I had let him keep it in my new garage.

I shook my head. No, I knew exactly why I'd done it. He'd needled me, pressed me, and annoyed me to the point where I had just given in. Like I had so many times throughout our relationship. Most times, I didn't even realize what had happened until it was too late. Like when he had been laid off from his other realtor firm when the housing market went bust, and I had given in to him taking some time off to figure out what he wanted to do. Or when he'd tried to open up his own firm and failed. I gave in then, too, and had been okay with him taking out a loan in both of our names because he was my husband. And I thought he knew best.

Thank God he had paid that off eventually. Thank goodness none of his debt was now in my name.

Because divorce hurt your credit, and I wanted nothing to do with Nicholas.

Thank God he hadn't been on the deed to the bakery. I had gotten it on my own, mostly because I had been working for another bakery, so I had full-time income and a successful business plan. It hadn't made sense to put Nicholas on the business since he wasn't working for me.

Maybe some part of me had always known that things might get worse between us as time moved on. I didn't know. All I did know was that I was beyond grateful that he couldn't touch my future. I loved cake decorating. I adored making things for people that made them smile. And I loved baking things that tasted amazing.

Nicholas had never understood any of that.

He had always thought my baking was a hobby. But I made money on the side, moonlighting while working for other people.

I always had an extra cushion, so when Nicholas lost his job, we were okay. Things had been tight, sure, but we had been okay.

And things were okay now. Things weren't as tight, even though I lived like they were.

And taking a day off for myself was good for my health.

Apparently, Nicholas was moving into a larger home and would have space for his stuff now. That meant he would finally take the boxes in my garage. Things I really wanted to burn or just toss into the garbage. Or, hell, give it all to charity as a donation and see what was in them. Because I hadn't even opened them to peek.

Once or twice, I had thought that maybe there was drugs or something in them. Because I still didn't know if him snorting coke off Becca's boobs had been the first time or the last time or one of many. But a friend who had a canine drug dog had let him sniff around the boxes, and he hadn't detected anything. I didn't know if that was entirely on the up and up, but I hadn't cared. I didn't want to open them. Didn't want to see evidence of any other secrets that might destroy another piece of me. Because I had been holding onto the parts of myself that I still had with broken fingernails as it was. I had been clawing to hold onto that remaining part of my soul. And I hadn't wanted to tarnish anything else, didn't want to lose anything else by opening a box. So, a friend had helped a bit. And based on that experiment, I didn't think there were drugs in there. Because, hell, that would just be one more thing Nicholas would have tried to fuck me over with.

Before I could get myself worked up to a good mad again, the doorbell rang, followed by three sharp raps. A pause, and then four more knocks.

Nicholas was always in a hurry. Unless others were waiting for him, then he took his time. But when it was his time, everyone had to move fast for him. I hadn't minded when we were younger because I had liked to move quickly, and things had made sense.

In retrospect, nothing had made sense. But there was nothing I could do about it now.

I took my time opening the door, maybe a little passive-aggressively, but this was my house. And I would not let Nicholas ruin this space with his energy. In fact, he didn't even have to walk in the door. And I was going to make sure he knew that. I had reminded him of that on the phone, and he had been short and terse with me. He would just have to deal. I didn't know when he had fallen out of love with me. I didn't know when he had turned into the person he was today. But I didn't want anything to do with him. Not anymore.

I opened the door and held back a grin as his hand stalled up in the air, probably readied to knock again, this time a little harder most likely. Maybe he would have even shouted my name. That would have been great for the neighbors. "Erin!" That loud voice of his would have carried to the neighbors', and I would have had to deal with it later. Yay. He really just needed to leave. Maybe I should have given all of his stuff to Goodwill.

"It's about time. Why the hell did you keep us waiting?"

"Hello, Nicholas." I tried to smile, attempted to be peaceful, but then I realized that he had just said the word *us*. I turned to the left ever so slightly and did my best to keep the smile on my face. I would not be the bitter ex-wife. I would not become the person he wanted me to be. I would be the Erin *I* wanted to be. The woman I needed to be. "Hello, Becca."

He had brought the cocaine-laden ex-cheerleader.

When had my life become a cliché? I wasn't sure. But it was probably when Becca had shown up in it.

No, I would not blame her. Not her alone anyway. Nicholas had been the one to dip his dick in something he shouldn't have. He was the one who'd failed us. Maybe some of the responsibility was mine, but the pain I felt was all on him.

Though I refused to become bitter because of it.

"Seriously, Erin. I don't know why you have to be this way. Come on now." Nicholas tried to shoulder past me, but I stood my ground. Just folded my arms over my chest and stayed in the way of the door. "Your stuff's in the garage, Nicky. You don't need to come inside."

I hadn't even realized that I had let the word *Nicky* past my lips until I saw his eyes narrow. His cheeks went ruddy, and his jaw tightened.

Nicky. Exactly what Devin had called him. Maybe it was a little petty of me, but I couldn't help it. He had brought Becca to my home. A place he had never shared with me. It made absolutely no sense other than for the fact that he wanted to rub her in my face. Frankly, the thought made me shudder. I didn't want her rubbing anything on me. At all. So...no. I really didn't want him in my space. I just wanted him gone. And I wanted to talk to Devin.

I quickly quashed that thought. I had been with Devin one night. I had gone on exactly one date, and I had initially met him again by humiliating myself in front of him. There was no way I would rely on him like that. I needed to depend on myself. I couldn't put my faith in anyone else.

"What the hell did you just call me?" Nicholas asked through gritted teeth.

"Your stuff's in the garage." I wasn't going to touch on his name. I hadn't meant to call him that. I didn't want to be that person. It had just slipped out. I'd always thought it was weird that he liked being called Nicholas and hated being called anything else. But it was his name, and I wasn't going to be rude or annoying about it. I needed to be the bigger person. I hoped. Maybe.

"You're not even going to let us inside?" he asked.

"That's what she said," Becca said, looking down at her phone. "Just get your shit and let's go. I don't even know why I had to come here. She shouldn't even have your stuff anyway. I mean, who wants to live in this hell-hole?" She rolled her eyes, looking much like she had when she was eighteen and not like a woman who was now in her twenties. It was exhausting.

"When did we become a cliché, Nicholas?" See, I'd gotten the name right that time. I was not going down that road. But I really hadn't wanted to ask that question. It just slipped out. I just wanted him off my property, and out of my face. And, maybe, even out of my life entirely. But while

Denver might be a big city, it still felt like a small town sometimes. I couldn't avoid him forever unless I moved. And there was no way I was doing that.

"A cliché? You want to talk about clichés? You're the cliché. You were always a frigid bitch. Why do you think we're divorced?"

"Excuse me?" I asked, my voice frosty. Huh, I guess I *was* frigid.

"You heard me. You were always a little nothing. You never wanted to be at my level. That's why I had to look elsewhere. You didn't see the big picture. You just wanted to go home and bake and be a fat-ass in the kitchen. Whatever. I had plans. Things that didn't include you. But you had to get all uptight and be a bitch about it. Because of that, you took half of everything. Everything that was mine. I worked my life for this, and you just took it all. So, yeah, I'm getting my fucking shit out of your garage, and it's all because of you. You're the one who did this."

I didn't actually think the phrase *seeing red* was real. But it was like a haze had moved over my eyes. I couldn't quite comprehend what had just happened. This wasn't the man I married. This was not the guy I had loved for so many years of my life. This was not the man who was my only love.

What the hell had happened to him?

Maybe that line of coke had fucked him up. Or perhaps he was always this bad deep down. Maybe losing his job and losing so much outside of that had done this. I didn't know. But I knew I didn't want any part of it.

"How did this happen?" I asked in a whisper. Damn it. I was exhausted. I had to stop letting my thoughts out like that.

"Maybe if you hadn't put so many expectations on me, it wouldn't have been an issue." He spat out the words, and I involuntarily took a step back. "Perhaps if you had realized I wasn't the ten-year-old you met on the bus, this wouldn't be a problem. But, whatever. Becca and I are going to get married. And I'm going to finally get what I deserve. You do you, Erin."

"Oh," I whispered. Trying to swallow hard. I had put expectations on him? Like having a job? No, I wasn't going to say that out loud. I wasn't going to extend this. I couldn't prolong this. I just didn't understand what had happened. I did not know this man in front of me. Becca seemed completely disinterested, but I didn't care about her. They were going to get married? Fine. Maybe he could finally find what he wanted. Because, apparently, I wasn't it. Evidently, I had never been it.

I closed the door behind me and pushed past them so I could walk across my yard to the garage. I could have gone through the side, but I unlocked it instead and pressed a few buttons so the garage door opened. My car was inside, and his boxes were off to the side, taking up far too much space.

"There they are. I have a dolly too, but I'm going to need that back if you use it."

"I don't really give a shit." Nicholas pushed past me, and Becca trotted along, her attention focused on her phone.

She was dressed to the nines in high-heeled wedges with her hair teased out perfectly. She looked amazing. I wouldn't fault her for that. I *would* hold the cheating against her, but I didn't know her. Not really. I couldn't hate her. But I didn't want to be near her either.

I stood, watching to make sure Nicholas didn't take anything that wasn't his and then moved off to the side, trying not to stand in a defensive position. But I wanted this done. I just really wanted all of this done.

He finally put everything in the back of his SUV and slammed the hatch.

"That's all of it."

"Good. Have a nice life, Nicholas."

"You know what, God help any man you get your claws into."

My eyes widened, but I just stared at him. Who was this man?

"I was ten when we met, Nicholas. What kind of claws did I have?"

He just glared at me, and I was done. So done with this. This is why I didn't want another man. This is why I just wanted to be by myself and figure out who I was without him. So, I just took a step back and threw my hands into the air. "You know what? Fuck it. I'm out. You got your stuff. And we're done. Have a good life, Nicholas. You, too, Becca. I'm done."

Nicholas started growling something else, but Becca got into the passenger side of the SUV, and I walked away. I made sure the garage door was closed and locked before locking myself in my house.

The tears fell before I even realized they were coming, and I cursed at myself. I did not want to cry over Nicholas. I had cried enough. I had growled plenty. I had done so much because of him. And because of me. Because not all of this could be on his shoulders. I had been the one to marry him. I had missed the signs. And now, I had to live with the decisions.

I went to my bathroom and wiped my face, willing myself to calm down. I was tired. And I didn't even have time to really revel in what had happened the night before with Devin because I had to deal with Nicholas.

So much for taking time for myself, right?

As if the heavens knew that tonight would be a weird one, my phone buzzed. I looked down at the readout. Devin was calling.

Maybe I should answer. Perhaps I would do exactly what I had said I would. No emotion. No connections. Just friends. Friends with benefits. They did that in the movies. Maybe I could do that here. I wasn't going to think about the fact that it rarely worked out on the big screen. It could work out in real life. This wasn't fiction, after all.

I answered and smiled. Ignoring the stark look on my face in the mirror.

"Hey, I was just thinking about you."

"Yeah?" he asked, his voice a deep growl that went straight through me. "I think I was doing the same about you. Just wanted to see how you were this morning."

"I'm fine. Last night was amazing." I blushed, and just shook my head. He couldn't see me. But I had a feeling he knew that I was blushing.

"Yeah, it was. Do you want to go for a drink tonight? You said you weren't working today, but I know you're working tomorrow."

"I am, but I could maybe do something a little early." I didn't know if I was doing the right thing. But then again, I never knew if I was doing the right thing anymore.

"I can pick you up."

"That'd be great." I held back a sigh, collecting my thoughts. I needed to make sure everything was out in the air. It was good to be open and honest in any type of relationship. Even in this kind.

"So, we're still friends, right? Friends that are just doing this thing. I really have no idea what to say. I suck at this."

Devin was silent for so long that I was afraid I had said the wrong thing. Apparently, I was really good at fucking things up today.

"I know what you mean. And, yeah, it still works for me. I'll pick you up. Wear something hot."

I laughed and got the rest of the details before hanging up and looking down at my phone. Okay, then. I could do this. I wasn't going to lose myself in this. Everything could just be casual. I wouldn't fall. And I wouldn't get hurt. Because when I fell, I got hurt. And I refused to be that person again.

No matter the pain. No matter the cost.

Eight

DEVIN

I PULLED UP TO ERIN'S HOUSE AND TURNED OFF the engine, wondering if I was doing the right thing. I wasn't good about making decisions when it came to her.

Hell, she was hurting, and yet I just kept showing up. I kept being here. But she didn't want serious. Did I? I didn't know. But it was kind of weird going into this, knowing that it wasn't going anywhere.

Why was I so worried about my feelings in a relationship anyway? It wasn't as if I actually knew if I truly wanted to be serious or not. Just because Dimitri had been married once, had bitten off more than he could chew with his first wife yet now had the actual love of his life with the second, didn't mean I needed to get married.

Hell, Caleb and Amelia could each find their other halves before I did. And that would be just fine. Yeah, it would be nice to have someone to come home to. Nice to actually have something steady. But it wasn't going to be with Erin. She'd made that clear. And I had to be okay with that.

Because she wasn't anywhere near ready for a relationship. I didn't want to be her rebound. Even though I *was* her rebound. In every sense of the word.

We were even using the phrase: *friends with benefits.* Fuck buddies. That was fine. But I wouldn't be the rebound who wanted more. I couldn't let that be me.

I would just have fun. Make sure she knew that she could have fun, too. Go along for the ride.

Dimitri could be happy in his marriage. Amelia could finally tell Tobey that she loved him or whatever. And maybe Caleb would even find someone.

I snorted. Okay, maybe not Caleb. He was a little rougher, a little more dark and dangerous.

That made me crack up. Thinking of my brother as anything but my baby brother? Yeah, not so much.

I got out of the truck, patted my baby, and went to Erin's front door. She opened it as if she had been waiting for me. I didn't know how I felt about that. Because I kind of *wanted* her to be waiting for me. I wanted her to be looking out the window and watching for me.

But I had to back the fuck up right there with those thoughts. Because she wasn't mine. She couldn't be mine.

I needed to remember that.

"You look great," she said, grinning. I looked down at what I wore. I'd pulled on some jeans I'd only worn once that were a little tight around my thighs and butt. But, apparently, they looked good. I'd also pulled on a black T-shirt, one that fit my arms but showed off the ink on both of my sleeves. I didn't show off my ink too often. Even when it was fucking hot outside. I tried not to look too dangerous when I was dealing with the mail. After all, I had to be the friendly mailman. I couldn't look like some degenerate criminal.

Not that people with tattoos or piercings were degenerate criminals. But I couldn't help what people thought. I had a big beard that was still within the dress code of my job. But I didn't look like a typical mailman. Whatever that meant. And that was fine by me. I liked my ink, and I knew I would likely add more. I went down to a little shop in Denver called Montgomery Ink, and an equally big, bearded dude named Austin took care of me there. His sister, Maya, had done a few tattoos on my back, as well, but Austin usually handled my projects. Although now that I thought about it, I should probably go down south to Colorado Springs where my big brother was.

Dimitri had married into the Montgomerys, a twist of fate that I hadn't really figured on happening. But considering that there were like a thousand Montgomerys in the world, someone was bound to marry into the family. But Dimitri's wife's sister and brother owned another tattoo shop called Montgomery Ink Too down in Colorado Springs. Apparently, they were connected or something. Maybe Austin would let me go down there and see what my new family could do.

I pushed those thoughts out of my mind because all I really wanted to do was look at the woman in front of me. She had on tight jeans that looked as if they were painted on with these black and wood-looking wedges, her little red toenails peeking out of the front. With that, she had on a black tank that dipped into a deep V and showed off her magnificent cleavage. And it looked like one of those halter things that I figured would show off some of her back.

It made me want to lick her skin. It made me want to strip off each piece of clothing and maybe just fuck her wearing those shoes and nothing else.

Yeah, that would be good.

I cleared my throat. "You look good, too."

She blushed and looked down at her hands before playing with her purse. "You were silent for so long, I was afraid I wore something wrong."

She tucked a piece of her blond hair behind her ear, and I noticed that she wore these dangling earrings that seemed to have a hoop within a hoop. I didn't really understand how it worked, but they looked nice. I reached out and flicked one. "Nice."

She laughed. "They looked good in the store. I went to this little boutique called Eden off the 16th Street Mall."

I grinned wide. "I know the owner. She's married to my tattoo artist."

"Small world." I've always wanted to go in there and get a tattoo for myself."

I licked my lips and ran my gaze over her bare skin. Or at least what she was showing me. I wanted more. Damn it. I had to push that thought out of my head. I just wanted to fuck her. That was it. Fucking and friends. That was all I needed.

"Well, I'll take you whenever you want to go. They have a long waiting list, but I'm kind of family now."

"What do you mean?"

"Come on, get in the truck and I'll explain."

I walked her over, loving the way she let me put my hands around her hips to help her hop in. Sure, she could have done it on her own. But I liked helping. Any excuse to get my hands on her, right?

"Anyway, my older brother, Dimitri? He married Thea Montgomery. She's part of the Montgomery family that runs the other Montgomery tattoo shop down south in Colorado Springs. Cousins to those who run the shop in Denver."

"Oh, wow. I love all the connections. So, are you going down there to get your tattoos now?"

"I was literally just thinking about that. I might. I mean, Austin might tan my hide for that, but it could be worth it. I hear every single one of them is amazing."

Her gaze raked my arms, and she licked her lips. Yeah, it was going to be really hard to drive with a hard-on. But every time I thought about Erin, especially in those wedges of hers and nothing else, I got a hard-on. So I was being pretty good about driving and trying not to look like my dick was pressing through my jeans.

"They do good work."

"So, what are you thinking about getting?" I asked, pulling onto the freeway.

"I don't know. I was thinking some kind of tree with some ravens on my shoulder. I know it seems almost cliché now. But I like it. It's strong, and it'll be there for ages. Even when the leaves fall, the branches will always be there. And it grows over time. Plus, I've always loved ravens. If I could have a pet one I would, but I don't want to be too weird."

I looked over at her and smiled. "That'd be cool actually."

"I'm so not home enough for that, though. And that's not really a thing."

"It could be."

"You're right. But I'm fine just watching them from afar. Crows and ravens seem to follow me wherever I go. I used to think that was an omen, but now I think they're just protecting me. Or maybe I just get a little tired, and I want to think something makes sense and means more when it's just birds that happen to live near me."

I reached out and gripped her hand. Our fingers tangled, so I kept them there on the console, grateful that she didn't pull away. We were friends. Friends who fucked. And that was fine. But I wanted to touch her.

All it did was bring on the anticipation of later, right?

"I think if you need to see signs, then they're there. And there's nothing wrong with wanting them. There's nothing wrong with believing that what you need is out there. I see crows and ravens all the time when I'm out on the job. They're pretty magnificent. Even if that movie, *The Birds*, kind of ruined them for a lot of people."

"They get such a bad rap. If anything, it's pigeons. Pigeons are the devil."

She said it with such vehemence, I laughed. "Yeah, I can see that. Especially when they're downtown. They just lower their heads and charge."

"I know!" she said on a laugh.

I pulled into the lot of a local bar, one where I could have just a drink and then keep driving. It wouldn't put me over the legal limit, and I felt safe to do so.

It wasn't the same place I had seen her in the sparkly dress. I didn't want to bring those memories back. And, frankly, I didn't want her to think of her ex while she was with me. Call me a selfish bastard, but whatever. We might just be friends, we may be doing whatever without strings, but I didn't want that layered on top of it all. Even though it was as if it were already cooling to my skin.

Because no matter what happened, Erin would see this relationship, and maybe any she had in the future, with a film of Nicholas over it. There was no getting around that. Hell, I would always have my ex-girlfriends in the back of my mind. Even if none of those relationships were as serious. Even if I hadn't been hurt like Erin had. There'd always be some form of comparison there. There had to be. It was only human.

It didn't mean I had to like it, though.

I hated it, actually. Fucking hated it.

I went around and helped her out of the truck, her body sliding slowly down mine. I swallowed hard, my cock pressing against her belly. Her eyes widened, and I knew she felt it.

I cleared my throat. "Hell, it's hard to stay sane when I'm around you."

"I'm going to take that as a compliment," she said with a laugh.

I lowered my head and brushed my lips against hers. Just a soft caress, one that sent a shot of need down deep in my belly and pebbled her skin.

I slid my hands down her arms just to warm her up and then pulled away.

"Can't keep doing that in public. If I do, I'll probably get a ticket for indecent exposure." I adjusted myself behind my jeans, grateful that at least these weren't too tight in the groin. I was going to hurt myself one day because of her.

Maybe I was going to get hurt because of her no matter what.

Fuck. Where had that thought come from? What we had didn't mean anything serious. I didn't need to think past what we had now. I had done something like this before. No strings, just friends, just sex. I could do it again.

Erin wasn't anything special.

And that was the biggest lie I had ever told myself. Hell.

She ran her hands down the front of her shirt, and it tugged the top of it down just enough that more of her tits showed. I groaned and then closed my eyes. "You really have to stop playing with your shirt like that. It's getting really difficult to think and function with all of my blood going down to my cock."

She flushed and threw back her head as she laughed. "I can't with you."

"What is that supposed to mean?"

"You know what you're doing. You're getting me all hot and bothered, and now we're going into a bar. How am I supposed to get thoughts of going down on you out of my mind?" Her eyes widened, and she slammed her hand over her mouth.

I stood there, stunned for a minute, and then *I* was the

one who threw back my head and laughed. "Jesus Christ, woman."

"I cannot believe I just said that. I don't think I've ever said anything like that in my life."

"Well, I liked it. So, if me thinking that you look hot as fuck is going to make you talk like that? I'll keep going."

"I mind."

I frowned. "What do you mean?"

"Oh, I don't mind talking like that in private. Even though I don't really do that. Ever. But what if someone had heard?"

I looked around at the empty parking lot. "I wouldn't have kissed you like that, wouldn't have looked at you the way I was in public if we weren't alone. Well, I might, but it wouldn't be on purpose. I'm not going to embarrass you, Erin. I'm not going to make you feel like people are watching you to the point of you being uncomfortable. Ever. Got me?"

She studied my face for so long, I was afraid I had said something wrong. Hell, she thought she was having issues with relationships? I had no idea what I was doing.

"I believe you."

I sighed out in relief and then grabbed her hand. "Come on, let's get a drink. And not think about blowjobs."

She snorted, and I almost tripped over my feet. "Devin!"

"What? I can't help it."

"So you say."

"Yeah, I think we're pretty poor influences on each other."

"I don't mind."

I gave her hand a squeeze, and then we made our way through the front door and into the bar. It wasn't a dive bar, but it wasn't in a popular, touristy area either. It was just a nice place where I knew some of the guys, and all of us took care of each other. I waved to a few people, but it was pretty quiet. We took a seat in the corner, but still at the bar. And I ordered two beers.

"You don't want anything else?" I asked.

"No. I'm good with just a beer. I wasn't really planning on going out tonight."

"Well, I'm glad you said yes," I said. "I had a long day, and I'm going to have an even longer day tomorrow. And I just wanted to see what you were up to."

"That's very sweet."

The bartender set down our beers, and we clinked glasses before taking a sip. The amber ale slid down my throat, cooling my parched tongue, but it didn't quench my thirst.

I was afraid nothing but Erin could do that for me.

Well, fuck.

"So, what is up with you? You want to talk about what put that tone in your voice when I called?"

She looked down at her glass, playing with the condensation with the tips of her fingers. "Nicholas came by."

"Are you okay?" I asked, leaning forward.

Her eyes widened, and she shook her head and then nodded quickly. "Oh, I'm fine. I didn't mean it like that. He came by to get his stuff."

"He had stuff at your place?"

"Yeah. Stuff he couldn't fit in his new condo. But because he's moving in with Becca, you know the woman that he cheated on me with? Apparently, they're getting married and moving into a house. So he needed his stuff. Anyway, I don't even know why I said I would take care of it all this time, but I did. Stupid me. Either way, it's gone now. But he said a few things I don't even want to get into. I just hate the fact that he makes me so angry. And bitter. I don't want to be that woman. I don't want to be someone who thinks about him like that. That puts him in every single conversation. Exactly what I'm doing right now. And he's not worth it."

"You're not that woman. He was a big part of your life. And he happened to be a part of your day. Of course, you're going to think about him." That didn't mean I didn't want to break the asshole's nose. What a fucking prick.

"I guess that makes sense. I just hate the way he makes me feel. And then I hate the fact that I let myself feel that way. I go on and on about finding this new me and trying to figure out my own path, and then I get angry thinking about him. About what he did to me. And what part I played in that."

"Don't tell me you blame yourself."

"Maybe a little. Maybe I should've walked away sooner. I don't know. But it's over, and I don't want to think about it anymore. Because I'm happy. I love my job. I have friends now that aren't connected to him."

"Like me?" I asked, not knowing why I'd said the words.

She smiled then, her eyes darkening. "Like you. I like you, Devin Carr. I just want you to know that." I leaned forward and tucked her hair behind her ear. "I like you, too." I watched her throat work as she swallowed hard until I leaned back and took a sip of my beer. I needed to think, focus. Because going down on her on the bar top would probably get me sent to jail. But damn it, it would probably be worth it.

"Anyway, I don't want to be the center of the universe, so tell me what's up with you," she said quickly after taking a sip of her beer.

I shrugged. "Nothing really. You know my job. You know my family."

"Not really. You dated Jennifer a long time ago. And I know you have three siblings. But what do they do?"

I smiled. "Well, Dimitri's a teacher. He works down in Colorado Springs. And then there's my sister-in-law Thea, who I mentioned earlier. They're happy and probably thinking about babies if they're not already pregnant."

"Oh, really? You don't have any nieces and nephews yet?"

I shook my head. "Not that I know of."

She snorted at that. "It's a possibility?"

"Well, Caleb did have a wild streak at one point."

"Oh my God. I really hope that's not the case."

"I don't think so. My dad might've been many things, but he was really good at making sure we wrapped it up."

She opened her mouth as if to venture into the touchy subject of my father. I had left the door wide open, after all, but she just shook her head ever so slightly. I knew she wasn't going to move closer to that. Not yet. Was it because she didn't want to get to know me like that? Or was it because she knew it was a touchy subject? Knowing Erin, I had a feeling it was the latter. I didn't know why. Maybe it was just what I wanted to tell myself.

"Anyway, I have a nephew, but he's a dog. Captain. A very amazing Golden Retriever that's getting a bit older."

"Oh, I love Golden Retrievers. I wish they could live to be like fifty, though."

"I know, right? They're like the best dogs. I've always wanted one, but I'm not home enough." I shuddered. "Okay, I've always wanted a pet. Not a dog."

That made her laugh. "What do you mean by that?"

"I'm a mailman. We don't like dogs."

She looked at me, her eyes wide, and then she broke out laughing. I did, too.

"You're not serious."

"Not really. I am more of a cat or like a fish person, though. But I love Captain, just saying."

"You had me going there for a minute."

"Well, I try. As for other kids in the family, seriously, none that I know of. Caleb's not in a relationship, and I don't think he's ever been in a serious one. He's usually on location in Alaska or other remote places."

"What do you mean by that?"

"He's a boilermaker."

"A what?"

"He assembles, installs, and prepares boilers and vats and huge containers. All that stuff. So, he used to be constantly off on location, working on things that I have no idea what they do. But now he's back in Denver and staying for a bit. He's actually moving to construction. Don't really know why, maybe because he's getting a bit older. Not that he's old, considering he's my baby brother."

"True," she said, nodding. "And Amelia's not dating anyone that I know of, right? Or is she dating Tobey."

"I have no idea. Are they dating? Maybe. It's not like I can ask, because if I try to ask her about her love life, she rips me a new one, and I'm really tired of getting my ass beat by my little sister."

"Well, little sisters do need their privacy."

"Yeah, maybe I should go talk with Jenn about the perils of having a little sister."

"Maybe I don't want the two of you in the same room. I don't really want any reminiscing."

I knew she was teasing, but with the whole cheating thing with her ex? I was going to nip that in the bud right here. "Jenn and I were over a long time ago. I don't even feel like it's the same lifetime."

"Oh, I know. I didn't mean anything by it. I'm totally with you there. Don't worry, I'm not going to confuse you with Nicholas. I promise."

"Good."

"Oh, did I tell you I called him Nicky to his face today?"

I grinned hard. "You didn't."

"I did. He got so mad. I have no idea why I did it. I think he just got into my head."

"Well, if he's an asshole to you, you call him Nicky."

"You know, I just might. I told myself that I didn't want to stoop to his level, but maybe just that one thing could make it better."

I clinked my glass to hers. "That's my girl."

She smiled, and I swallowed hard. Because she wasn't my girl. Sure, maybe for the night. But outside of that? We drank another drink, sharing a second beer so I could drive, and we just had eyes for each other. No one else. Yeah, some of my friends came in, but they didn't come to me. I didn't bring girls to this bar. It was my comfortable bar. Not that I was a big drinker, but I didn't like to always sit at home alone to have my beer. I liked to be around people.

I liked being around Erin.

We paid our tab, and I drove her home, both of us holding hands, a little quiet, a bit tense. But my dick was hard, and her breaths were coming in little pants.

Because it was a little touch here, a brush there, a small breath, a quiet moan. We weren't even kissing. We were barely touching.

On the way back to her place, there was a little rock quarry that didn't have security, and I knew some of the workers out there. I knew it would be empty at this time of night, and I just wanted to see what she would do. We didn't have to do anything, but if she said yes? I just wanted to know.

So, I pulled over, turned off the engine, and looked at her.

She looked out the window and slowly turned back to me. "This doesn't look like where you live, Devin."

"I just wanted to kiss you. Is that okay with you?"

"Do you have to ask?" she asked.

"Yeah, with you? I always will."

"Then kiss me."

I moved forward, slowly tracing my finger along her jaw, and then I lowered my lips to hers.

It was a soft kiss, just a brush of mouths, but then she parted her lips, and there was no stopping either of us. I groaned into her, tugging the back of her hair so I could wrench her neck to the side. I deepened the kiss, undoing her seatbelt at the same time. She moved one of her hands between us, gripping my erection through my jeans, and I groaned.

Somehow, my hands moved in between us, working on her pants, tugging them down ever so slightly so I could get behind the waistband.

"Devin, I need you."

"I just need to touch you. I don't think my truck is conducive to sex, but I just need to touch you."

"Okay. Anything."

"That's the magic word." I slid my hand inside her panties and over her mound, cupping her.

She went still, shivering in my hold. I slowly ran my middle finger over her tight nub, the wetness of her already so potent I almost came in my jeans. I rolled her clit between my fingers and then slid my hand deeper, her jeans pressing tightly against the back of my hand so it was hard to work, but I could get at least one finger along her slit. I moved up and down slowly with each kiss, with each thrust of my tongue. She panted, her hands trying to reach my belt buckle, but I knew this wasn't about me.

I slid one finger into her and curled it, slowly running my forefinger along her clit, and my middle finger along that sweet bundle of nerves.

She stiffened in my hold, and then she came, her cunt squeezing my finger hard.

She panted, her whole body shaking, and then I looked at her. Her eyes were so dilated, I knew she had come hard.

I slid my finger out of her, slowly rubbing over her clit again until she shivered, and then I put my digits in my mouth to lick them clean.

"That was...I never go off that quick."

"Good to know."

And then she grinned and went back to my belt buckle. I leaned back and let her work. She slowly undid my zipper, and I rotated my hips so she could get better access.

"You don't have to do this if you don't want," I whispered.

"No, I want this. And you're not going to die on me."

"That's my girl."

Again, she wasn't my girl, but I couldn't think about that. Not with her hand on my dick and her mouth on the tip.

She had pulled me out when I wasn't looking, and now slowly bobbed her head over me. I slid my hands into her hair, slowly guiding her as she squeezed the base of my dick, sliding up and down, her mouth enveloping me in a warm caress.

She moved quicker, hollowing her mouth as her tongue played with the tip, and I knew I wouldn't last long. I slid my hand through her hair, the other down her back to her butt. I squeezed one cheek and then slid my hand in between her legs and over the seam of her pants so I could rub on her clit. I rubbed hard, just enough to get her going, but I was the one who came. I tried to pull back, attempted to warn her, but she clamped down on me, taking every ounce of me. Licking me up as if I were an ice cream cone.

Jesus Christ. It was like I was a fucking teenager, thinking of her like that.

But a blowjob in my truck?

Yeah, that was a fantasy from my teens. And, apparently, a fantasy for now, too.

Jesus.

She pulled away, licking her lips and wiping off her chin. I grimaced, leaned forward, then kissed her hard. And grinned.

"You are one hell of a woman."

She smiled, her eyes dancing.

"And you are one hell of a man."

"I've got tissues to clean this up," I said quickly.

"Okay. And then can we go to your house? Or should we go to mine? Because I don't think we're finished yet."

I cupped her face, running my thumb over her cheek.

"No, Erin. We're not done by a long shot."

As soon as I said the words, I hoped I wasn't wrong. I hoped I wouldn't hurt us both. But I had a feeling there wouldn't be any easy answers no matter what happened. For either of us.

NINE

ERIN

HORROR.

Absolute horror.

That's what I faced as soon as I took my first step into my kitchen.

Dear. God.

Drip. Drip. Drip. Drip.

My hands shook as I tried to take in what was in front of me, my mouth going completely dry. I swore I had to be seeing things. I *had* to be seeing things.

"Oh my God," I whispered and then pulled myself out

of whatever hysteria I was slipping into. I could not freak out. But I really wanted to freak the fuck out just then.

It had been raining all evening, to the point where there had been flash flooding in the area. I was very lucky that my house was on a slight hill so I didn't have to worry as much as some other people. At least, at my home.

But at my place of business? Oh my God.

The back of my kitchen was flooded. It looked as if a lake had poured in, and I could barely breathe.

No, I didn't think I was actually breathing.

I rubbed my hand over my chest, trying to calm whatever was going on inside me, but I swore I could hear my heart beating so rapidly in my ears, it was like an echo that would never end.

I looked up at the ceiling and tried to formulate a plan. The recessed ceiling had been torn away in chunks where the water dripped in, and it looked as if it had been pouring in at one point.

This wasn't a pipe. No, it was from the roof itself. My building was only one story with nothing on top of it. So, whatever had come in through the roof had happened from the storm itself. Or that, combined with wear from over the years.

And the deluge happened right on all of my materials.

And the worst part? It wasn't just in the kitchen area.

As soon as I saw the two inches of water on the floor and all over my pristine counters and everything else, I screamed, turned off the power, and ran back to check the fridge. The cake that I had spent hours of my life on, the one that was more important than anything to me at that moment because of the clients and the wedding that was happening the next day, was in there.

But what I was looking at just then...

It didn't resemble a cake.

It didn't resemble anything.

"Oh my God," I repeated, my hands shaking.

Somehow, part of the fridge itself had caved in, even though it was stainless steel and metal and had layers of insulation. But the flood itself had dented it, so a stream of water had dripped in, right on my cake.

The project had been beautiful, white fondant with hand-strung lace all around it. I had spilled edible, blue flowers all over it. Meaning, I had painstakingly handcrafted each petal, the blue the perfect shade to match the groom's eyes.

I had stared at that groom's face in a photo for days, making sure that I got it right. Because that was the same dye lot number of the bridesmaids' dresses. The blue of almost everything. Because the bride loved her soon-to-be husband so much, she wanted him everywhere. He hadn't made any decisions about the wedding, it had all been the bride. And she had pulled her groom into everything.

And now the cake looked like the corpse bride.

The lace had bled into itself, the blue bleeding, as well. It looked as if blue streaks were pulsating down the lace, like the blue veins of a zombie corpse bride. This wasn't the wedding of the moment, this was the wedding from hell.

"Oh my God!" Zoey screamed from the back door. I tried to shout her name, attempted to tell her where I was.

But as I opened my mouth, nothing came out.

Nothing was working.

My hands were numb, my brain wasn't firing, but I could do this. I could do this on my own. I could fix this. I could remake this cake. I could call the insurance adjusters. I could clean this up. I could do it all.

So why wasn't I breathing?

Why was this happening at all?

Oh, God. Everything from my life had been put into this. My life savings, my retirement. This was my business. This was the one thing I had left after the divorce. Now, it was gone. Just like the death of that cake in front of me.

"Oh my God. The cake. It looks like a corpse. You know, like that Tim Burton movie? *The Corpse Bride.*"

I turned on my heel, ignoring the splash of water as I did.

"Why was that the first thing I thought, too?" I asked, putting my hands over my eyes.

"I can't think. I need to turn off the water. But it's not water, is it? It's not a pipe. It's rain."

I lowered my hands. I looked at Zoey.

She shook her head, and tears fell from her eyes.

"No. It's not. Okay. I know the rain was bad. We can fix this. I know a clean-up crew. You call the insurance people, and then we'll worry about everything else. Call in your staff. I'll get Amelia in here. We'll figure it out."

I wasn't crying. I wasn't really doing anything. I was just standing there. And I couldn't just stand there. I needed to make decisions. I needed to take this into my own hands and figure it out because I had to do this alone. I could do this. I was strong. I was capable. I could do anything I set my mind to.

And I could not serve up a corpse bride cake.

"Why can't I get Tim Burton out of my head?" I asked. Knowing I was becoming a little hysterical. Okay, maybe a lot hysterical.

"Because it looks just like her dress. But that's fine. You're going to call the bride and let her know what happened."

"Oh my God. She's going to die."

"No. The cake is. But that's fine. You can do another one.

"The wedding is tomorrow."

Zoey just kept nodding. Her eyes wild.

"Oh. I know. But you can bake at home."

"I can't."

"Yes, you can. Stop it. Snap out of it."

"You sounded exactly like Cher the way you said that. You know, from that '80s movie?" Because she had. I snorted, and then I laughed. And then tears fell, and I hated myself for it.

Zoey stepped forward, her hands out, and I shook my head.

"No. Don't come at me, or I'm going to start crying again or harder, and I don't have time for that."

"Okay. We're going to clean this up. We're going to make lists. And we're going to figure this out. We're fine. Everything's going to be fine."

"Okay, yes, I totally believe you. But first, come on, let's get out of the fridge and, you know, out of this water because you're starting to make sounds that only dogs can hear at this point."

"True."

"Oh God."

"Darling? Erin?"

"Mrs. Murphy!" I said, pushing past Zoey and giving her a quick squeeze on the shoulder as I went to one of my neighbors. My shop neighbor, who sold pies. Actually, she was two buildings down, and our businesses didn't conflict with each other. I did mostly cakes and cupcakes and brownies. She did pies that she sold in the store rather than made-to-order like I did. We sometimes sold stuff together and worked with each other for different functions. I loved her to death. And for some reason, I just wanted to cry on her shoulder. Mrs. Murphy was in her late sixties, pretty, slender, and looked at least twenty years younger than she was. She had her hair bundled up in a bun on the top of her head. Her glasses were big and wide and the style that now fit the fashion, even though she had worn the same type when they weren't so in style.

"I was walking past this morning with my coffee and saw the outside of your building. Oh my God, darling. What can I do?"

"I don't know yet. But I might need your help. I have a cake due tomorrow, and I just don't know what to do."

"Well, first, you're going to call your insurance adjuster. And then you're going to come over to me, and we're going to get what you need done in my kitchen. I don't have all the pans that you need, but the water doesn't seem to have gotten to that side of your space, so we can move them over to mine, and we'll get it done. Between you and me and anyone else we can pull in from our staff, we'll get you set up. You just do what you need to do. Because you are going to be amazing."

"I don't...I don't know what to say," I said, my voice coming out in that high-pitched squeak again.

"You helped me when I broke my leg and couldn't keep up with orders. You worked day and night to make sure that I kept my business. And I'm going to do the same for you, young lady. You understand me?"

I couldn't say anything. Instead, the tears threatened again, but I refused to cry. Because if I cried, I wouldn't stop. And I needed to be stronger than that.

Zoey pushed past me and hugged the older woman.

"You're amazing, Mrs. Murphy. Okay, let's get this done. I'm going to call into my store and tell them I'm not going to be in today."

"You own the store, Zoey. You can't do that."

"I own the store, so maybe I can do exactly that."

"I can't ask that of you." I didn't want to take her away from her business. This was my problem.

"I can do whatever the fuck I want. And I know that look in your eyes. You're thinking that this is all your fault and your mistake, or some crap like that. And you're just going to shut up about that because I love you. This was an actual weather phenomenon. An actual and literal act of God. So you're going to shut the fuck up. And you're going to do what I say."

"I thought you just said that I was the boss of this place. You can't just take over."

"As soon as you breathe and stop freaking out, you are going to be your own damn boss."

"You know, I would chastise you both for your language, but I'll allow it for now," Mrs. Murphy said as she smiled at us.

I pulled my head out of my ass and rolled my shoulders back.

"Okay. Let's do this."

"See? Your voice is already lowering a bit, dear. Now only *some* dogs can hear you."

I flipped her off, cringed as Mrs. Murphy shook her head. And then got to work.

It took five hours. Five hours of dealing with phone calls, adjusters, emails, and crying brides.

But we were going to make it work.

Amelia had shown up during her lunch hour, complete with subs and sodas and chips for everyone, and rolled up her sleeves to help me with the fondant. While dealing with phone calls on my Bluetooth, my laptop in one corner, I baked my heart out.

The bride and I had come up with a plan, one where it wouldn't be as intricate, but would still be beautiful. I wasn't going to sleep that night, but I would get it done.

Between my staff, Mrs. Murphy's people, the woman herself, and my two friends, we were making it work.

I was still freaking out while trying not to think about the loss of revenue and the fact that I was going to have to borrow Mrs. Murphy's kitchen for longer than either of us planned. I wouldn't have a place to work until the insurance adjusters could finish their piece, and the contractors could come in and do the work. But I would make it work. I would just have to bake out of my home kitchen again just like I had when I first opened the business. I would figure it out.

Because there wasn't another option.

Zoey had come in with beautiful blue flowers that we were going to use around the base of the cake. I could replicate a lot of the edible flowers, but some of them would have to be real ones. The whole thing wouldn't be completely edible, but it would still be beautiful.

And the new cake wouldn't have as much lace, but I was going to do the top tier and the third tier down as all lace. The second and the base tier would have to be smooth fondant, but I was going to do my best to quilt some of it and add some edible pearls.

It would all work out. This wasn't going to be a complete corpse bride cake.

But the place that was my heart and soul, the business I had put so much of my life into, needed to be redone.

All because a storm had bulldozed its way through my roof and ruined everything.

I felt like I could barely catch my breath, but that was fine. I would make sure everything worked out.

It wasn't like I had another choice.

I was just working on another set of edible flowers when the door to Mrs. Murphy's pie shop opened, the bell signaling a customer. I froze when I heard a familiar voice.

A deep voice that went straight to my core and made my spine stiffen.

"Where is she?" Devin asked. I had my head and my back to the front as I worked on the flowers in my hands so I couldn't see him. I had to focus. I didn't have time for anything but this project.

But, damn, his voice did things to me.

"Erin? Are you okay?" he asked, coming to my side. I risked a glance at him, tried to smile. I knew it hadn't done its job when his brows rose.

"I'm fine."

"She's not fine, but at least her high-pitched-ness has gone down a bit. Both humans and dogs can hear her now."

"I would flip you off, Zoey, but my hands are full."

"I can see your hands are full," Devin said. "Why didn't you call me?" he asked, looking down at me with such a fierce expression, I turned away from it.

It was hard to focus when he was around. It was hard to do anything but want him when he was around.

And that was the problem.

"I...I didn't think about it."

"You didn't think about it."

I winced.

"I'm sorry. Everyone just showed up to help. I was doing fine on my own. I mean, I had to do this on my own. Maybe. But they came to me. And they're amazing. And I'm sorry. I just didn't think to call you." I winced again. "I mean, you don't work with cakes or anything."

"I don't. Neither does my sister. Or Zoey. And you don't have to do everything on your own, Erin."

Well, then. That was a verbal slap if I ever heard one. "I'm sorry," I said, shaking my head.

"I got it. You don't have to be sorry. But we're friends, too, right? Don't forget that. Now, tell me what I can do to help. And we'll get it done. You got a contractor to work on your place?"

"I do."

"It's a place you would have recommended anyway," Amelia said from across the kitchen.

"Good. Now, tell me what you need."

I just looked at him and wondered how this was my life now. I had so many people to rely on, so many people that hadn't been in my life before when I was with Nicholas.

I didn't know what to say, didn't know what to do. And I was afraid if I focused too hard, I would cry again. So, I pushed those thoughts out of my head and went to my mental checklist.

Being busy would help. And then I could think about my feelings.

Maybe.

Or maybe not.

TEN

DEVIN

———

I LEANED BACK AGAINST THE WALL AND EYED THE massive dog in front of me. Oh, it looked friendly. Generally, they all did.

It narrowed its dark eyes at me, and I tilted my head, trying to look calm. As if I weren't a threat. I wasn't a threat. The one with the very sharp teeth and shaggy head of hair, that one was the threat.

"Are you eying my dog?" Dimitri asked, walking into the living room with two beers in hand.

"You say dog, I say beast."

Captain, the very friendly and adorable, aging Golden

Retriever barked once, and then leaned in to my outstretched hand.

I wasn't afraid of dogs, not really. I had just been chased by one or two. And never by the big ones. No, it was always the small ones, the ones that made those yippy sounds. Yes, those were the ones that others in my profession called evil. They would latch onto your ankle just like in the media, and you'd have to shake them off. But you couldn't shake off poor Poopsie. Because if you did and you hurt it, it was your fault. Not the dog's, or the owners', who let the little rat come at you.

I pushed those thoughts from my mind, though, because now I was just ranting inside my head about invisible dogs that didn't actually exist. I was not afraid of dogs.

And I loved this one.

Captain had been in Dimitri's life for a while now, and he was sweet, caring, and seemed to know that I was slightly put off by the four-legged persuasion. He was always nice to me, and I was pretty sure he fucked around with me, as well. As in he slowly stalked me and narrowed his eyes at me, just to see what I would do.

But Captain was a good boy.

And I loved dogs.

I just didn't want one.

Maybe not until I retired.

"Captain, come here," Dimitri said, holding back a laugh.

I glared at my brother and held out my hand for the extra beer. "I don't hate your dog."

"I know you don't. And I know you've probably told yourself that in your head over and over again. But, really. It's like you want to be a stereotype."

I took a sip of my beer and pointed the neck of the bottle at my older brother. "It's not a stereotype if it actually happens. And, I'm pretty sure your dog just likes to mess with me."

"Yes, because he can totally do that." Dimitri met gazes with his dog, and I swore I saw a look of understanding there. Yep, they were messing with me. I seriously loved Captain. I loved all the sweet dogs that were in my life. I just didn't really like the yipping ones that attacked me when I was trying to deliver mail. But whatever. It was a hazard of the job and something I had to deal with. Daily.

"Anyway, thanks for inviting us all over for dinner," Dimitri said, petting Captain's head.

Captain had been named after Captain America. Dimitri and the new love of his life were equally addicted to all things Marvel. I didn't mind, but the fact that I had walked in on them in their kitchen at one point saying something about being on their left, and 'I love you three thousand,' and something else about pants being taken off and America's ass, I really wanted nothing to do with their fascination with Marvel.

I liked the movies, loved the comics, but I really had no idea how Marvel movies went with people's sex lives.

"I figured it was time for a family meal, and it's easier for you guys to come up here, rather than for us to go down there. But we'll take turns."

"Caleb's getting a bigger house, so we'll be able to fit all of us at some point."

"I know he's in the kitchen with Amelia and Thea, but do you know why he finally quit his job and is settling down here for another pension?" I asked, keeping my voice low.

"Nope. And I'm not going to ask."

I met Dimitri's gaze. "Really? You're not going to meddle?"

"I may be the big brother, but you're more meddling than I am."

"I'm not that bad," I said, scrunching my brow.

"You are that bad," Amelia said, walking in with a glass of wine in her hand. She'd tied her dark hair back from her face and put it into some kind of messy bun at the crown of her head. She was always working so hard these days. I rarely saw her. Though I had seen her the week before at Mrs. Murphy's bakery when I was there to try and help Erin, even though Erin hadn't wanted my help.

No, I wasn't going to be that person. At least, not now.

"Dimitri's worse than I am," I said quickly.

"Actually, you're pretty much the same."

"Hey," Dimitri and I said at the same time. We stared at

each other, clearly not knowing who should be more offended. It should be me. Right?

"Oh, come on, Dimitri lives in Colorado Springs so now he just FaceTimes and texts and calls to make sure that I'm doing what I need to and exhibiting proper behavior." Amelia rolled her eyes and took a sip of her wine.

"My honey bunny talking about proper behavior?" Thea said, walking in with a plate of cheese.

The fact that my brother's woman was holding a plate of cheese was not surprising in the least. I was pretty sure if cheese could be another part of their relationship, much like Marvel, they would be in some weird foursome that I wanted nothing to do with. They were both quirky and adorable. And I loved it.

It was good to see Dimitri happy. He hadn't been happy with his ex-wife. Not really. But none of us had said anything. Because it hadn't been our place. And, at the time, we had thought he was happy.

We'd been wrong. So wrong.

"Honey bunny?" Dimitri asked, raising a single brow. I couldn't do that. Apparently, it was hereditary, but only Dimitri could do it with that level of perfection. He must practice it in front of a mirror for hours. I wouldn't put it past him.

"What? I enjoy trying out new phrases. And you're just as bad as Devin. Caleb's pretty bad, too. As is Amelia." Thea just grinned as we all glared at her. "What? You all home in on each other's business, are all overprotective in different ways, and you want what's best for each other. It's like you're Montgomerys."

"We're Carrs," Caleb grumbled as he walked in, beer in hand. He leaned against the doorframe, a little separate from us but still part of the group. Classic Caleb.

"I know you're Carrs. I'm just saying that you're a very strong family. Therefore, you're always going to be in each other's business and wanting what's best for one another. Now, who wants cheese?"

"You know I do," Dimitri said, meeting Thea's gaze with a heated look.

"Okay, stop eye-fucking over the cheese," I grumbled, taking the plate from her.

"Now that's an image I never want in my brain again," Caleb said, snorting before taking a slice of Havarti and a cracker.

"There are four types of cheeses, but I have two spares if none of these work for you."

"So, you brought an entire smorgasbord of cheese to my house?" I asked, taking a bite of Brie on a piece of toasted bread. Thea had added a little bit of honey to the top, and I pretty much almost came in my jeans just then.

Dear God, I was becoming one of them with their cheese. I needed help. Or I just needed more cheese.

"Of course, I brought cheese," Thea said, giving me an innocent look. There was nothing innocent about any of us in the room. But that was fine. "Why would I leave the house without cheese?"

"Or baked goods," Amelia said, munching on a piece of aged cheddar. "She brought dessert."

"Well, you do own a bakery," I put in. "It's kind of your thing."

"And Erin's," Amelia said, batting her eyelashes.

"Erin? Who's Erin?" Thea asked.

"Erin Taborn. She used to be Erin Rose back in school." Amelia started talking, and I tried to shut her up, but she just turned her back to me so the rest of them were looking at each other, and I was left out. That way, they could talk about me. Ah, family.

"Wait, and you dated her sister, right? In high school?" Dimitri asked.

"Her name was Jennifer," Caleb put in.

I flipped them all off. "How on Earth do you know all that?" I asked, grumbling.

"Well, number one, Amelia knew. Therefore, we already sort of talked about it. But Thea didn't know. Now that she knows, we can all discuss your sex life." Caleb just grinned. "After all, we did see her sleeping on your couch."

"You made her sleep on your couch?" Thea asked.

"It was one time, and it was after she left her husband."

"Oh my God, Devin."

"Oh, stop it. That's not what I meant." I pinched the bridge of my nose. "I'm not getting into it."

"I will," Amelia said and then laid out all the facts as she knew them. It worried me how much she actually knew.

"And now her whole bakery is flooded?" Thea asked, her hands over her mouth. "Is there anything we can do? I mean, I know it's a bit of a drive down to mine, but maybe I can help. I don't even want to think about what would happen if that happened to my place." Dimitri leaned over and kissed the top of her head. "Considering that your bakery tried to go down in a blaze of glory, and you got hurt because of it, as did your brother-in-law? Let's not talk about what could happen to your bakery, okay?" Dimitri met her gaze, and we were all silent for a moment while the two of them just looked at each other.

The couple had gone through hell in order to get together, and I was glad that they had each other. And the fact that Thea was ready to help a woman that she really didn't know spoke volumes.

"Erin should be fine. It's been about a week now, and they've been working on things behind the scenes. She's been baking out of her kitchen and out of another company's kitchen, as well. It should only take another couple of weeks before things are back to normal. She's stressing, but she's getting stuff done."

"Oh, that's good to hear. But you let her know I'm here if there's anything I can do, any supplies or stuff that needs to be replaced that she can't get right now. I'm sure I have things that she could use."

"I'll let her know."

"You better."

"And you know, she's pretty much like you, Thea. She's probably not going to take help unless you push it on her. So, I'll keep a look out," Amelia said, smiling. "If it looks like she actually needs help and isn't going to take any, I'll push it at her."

"Hey, don't crowd her," I said, looking down at my beer.

"I'm not going to *crowd* her," Amelia said. "She's my friend. I want to help."

"Well, she's my friend, too. And she doesn't like asking for help." After all, she hadn't asked me for help at all. She hadn't even thought to contact me. No, everyone else had been there, helping her out. I hadn't been.

It still bugged the fuck out of me. Because even though we were just friends—friends with benefits, in fact—there should have been more in times like these.

I should have been able to help. But she hadn't wanted to rely on me.

And it grated.

"Friends?" Caleb asked.

"We don't have an exact label. She just got out of a very long-term relationship. A marriage that really didn't end well. And she doesn't want anything serious."

Everyone was silent for a moment, and Dimitri met my gaze, worry shining there.

"Well, what do you want?"

"I just want her happy," I whispered, not realizing the words were out until they were already there.

"So, what does that mean?" Amelia asked, coming over to put her hand on my forearm. "Because you need to be happy, too, Devin."

I snarled at them all and rolled my shoulders back. Even Captain leaned against me as if he knew I was feeling a little down. I didn't want them to see that. Dimitri might have been joking earlier, but I was the one who took care of people. Just like he was, but since he was down south, I was closer to the rest of the family. I had to be the strong one.

"I'm fine. We're only a few weeks in. It's not like there're wedding bells or some shit."

"Well, she does make wedding cakes," Caleb said, grinning.

"Yeah, not for herself. That's not happening." It wasn't going to happen. Especially if she had anything to say about it.

Not that I wanted to get married. But the idea that we were in such a murky relationship was weird. Because I did want to settle down eventually. I wanted a family. I looked at the way Dimitri was with Thea, the way they already had their dog and were thinking about babies. I wanted that.

It just wasn't going to happen with Erin.

So, I had to figure out what to do with that.

"I thought I was going to make all of your wedding

cakes?" Thea asked, putting her hands on her hips. "It was sort of the deal when I came into this family."

"Well, if we bring another baker into the family, we're going to have to have baking wars. Maybe we'll get a TV show," Amelia said, clapping her hands. "It would be fun."

"No baking wars," Dimitri said. "Plus, Thea's the best."

I raised both brows. "Yeah, pretty sure Erin's the best."

"Those are fighting words. And here I let you eat my cheese." Thea took the plate from me and lifted her chin. "There is no cheese for people who mock my baking."

"I didn't mock it. I just said Erin was superior."

"Because you're sleeping with her," Caleb said, reaching around Thea for another piece of cheese. "You have to say that."

"What, I like her goods."

"Oh, shut up," Amelia said. "That wasn't even a good joke."

"No, it really wasn't." I grinned and shook my head. "You're amazing, Thea. We'll just put you as equal. That way, I won't get kicked in the shin."

Thea raked her gaze down me, and then met my eyes. "Oh, I wasn't going to kick your shin, dear Devin."

I winced and covered myself. The rest of the room laughed.

We talked, and I just listened to my family and wondered how this had happened. I hated feeling insecure, hated feeling like I wasn't doing things right.

But it was fine. I could make Erin happy. If only for a little while.

And then I'd find what I needed. Find that time to settle down.

Because in the end, I was the one with my destiny in my hands. No one else.

And I wasn't going to get hurt. Nor was I going to let Erin get hurt. We'd figure it out.

At least, I hoped.

Eleven

Erin

I WAS EXHAUSTED DEEP DOWN TO MY BONES. BUT I was exhilarated at the same time. It had been two weeks since my shop ended up underwater. It was scary to think that I could have lost everything—and had lost some because of the rain. And a shoddy roof that shouldn't have been that shoddy.

The place had been inspected just this year, in fact, but they had either missed something, or the rain and wind had hit it just right.

The insurance adjuster hadn't been sure, but either way, I had gotten my money. I paid an expensive premium for a reason. Thankfully, I wasn't going to lose my entire life savings because of the damage.

Before, I likely would have freaked out more than I did. And I would have tried to lean on Nicholas. And he wouldn't have let me. He would've been focused on trying to find a job, trying to build a new business, trying to do something with him as the focus.

I hadn't realized until it was far too late how insular and selfish he actually was.

Everything I accomplished, I did on my own. Without him. Without his help. That was why my name had been on the deed, and he hadn't been part of it. He hadn't believed I could do it at all. He hadn't wanted us to spend any money on me, just him.

I hadn't realized that at the time. I'd only thought he hadn't wanted us to take the risks. Even though the entire way he operated was a risk.

But this wasn't that life. I wasn't with him. I never would be again.

And, thanks to my friends, especially Mrs. Murphy, I was doing okay. The damage hadn't been as bad as I thought, and the faulty refrigerator was being replaced. That meant I would soon be able to move back into my shop. In fact, they were talking about letting me go tomorrow. That's how fast everybody had worked for me. They were amazing. I honestly could not believe how many people cared about me now.

Especially Devin.

He was only supposed to be a distraction. Just fun.

But I was leaning on him. Relying on him. And it was scary.

Because what if he left? What if he decided that this was too much, just like Nicholas.

Just like my dad.

I shook my head, pushing those thoughts away. It wouldn't be good of me to dwell on them. Just because I was afraid of what might happen didn't mean it actually would.

After all, Devin and I had been very careful. We'd said we were just going to be casual. Sleeping with each other and going on dates when we could.

The fact that he was busy, and so was I, meant that we'd only seen each other a few times outside of him helping at the shop.

And that was fine.

I didn't need anything more. Because if I got more, I would want it. I would start to rely on it.

And I had to realize that I could only depend on myself.

The fact that I was also relying on my friends—Amelia, Zoey, Mrs. Murphy—notwithstanding. They were friends. They were different.

My sister Jennifer was far too busy with her family, and I didn't want to lean on her. I knew she would let me, but I wouldn't do it.

And Devin? Yes, he was a friend. But it was all so murky, I had to be careful. As long as we were cautious, no one would get hurt.

"What do you think about this dress?" Jennifer asked, holding up a very tiny little black dress to her body.

I grinned and shook my head. "Yeah, just think about one of your baby girls in that dress."

Jennifer raised her head and narrowed her eyes. "Excuse me? My babies are *way* away from wearing this type of dress."

"Yeah, not quite sure your ass is going to fit in that."

She flipped me off, and I just shook my head. "I'm kidding. Your ass is great. And even if your ass didn't fit in it, who cares. You could still wear it. Wherever you want. You're gorgeous, Jennifer."

"Aw, you're sweet. But, no, you're right. I don't think I can walk around the street with my ass hanging out. Literally. But maybe for at home with the hubby."

I mock-shuddered, and she just laughed at me. "You're ridiculous. I have baby girls. They did come from somewhere other than the stork. So, you know, I've had sex."

"I really don't want to think about it."

"So you don't want to think about the sex I've had with everybody? And not just my husband."

I froze.

Her eyes widened. "I meant before I met him. Not during. I'm not cheating on him. I swear. Oh my God. That just came out wrong. I was going to try to make fun of you and Devin being together. And then it got weird."

I just looked at her, blinking. "You wanted to try and make me think of you sleeping with the guy I'm currently sleeping with, and that wouldn't be weird?"

"Okay, I suck at these things. I'm not cheating on my husband. Nicholas is an asshole. I'm not." She paused. "Okay, so I am an asshole. But I'm your lovable asshole."

I just looked at her and threw back my head and laughed. "My lovable asshole?"

"What? It's a thing."

"It's really not. And I really don't want to know if you and Devin ever slept together."

"We didn't. If that's helpful. Although he is good with his hands."

She winked, and I gagged. "Hey. None of that now. I mean, if you keep going, I'm going to save that dress for when your oldest gets big enough to fit into it. And then she's going to show up wearing it to prom."

"Hey, you're supposed to be the cool aunt. Not the bad influence."

"I can be both."

"Like you have a bad bone in your body. You were the sweet and good one. I was the one with the rebellious side."

"Yeah, maybe. But look how good that turned out. I was the one in the nice and sweet and happy relationship since I was like ten or something. Now, look."

"You're a successful businesswoman with a group of friends and a steady life? I'm not quite sure what you're complaining about." She pulled out another dress, this one with sparkles, and then shook her head, tossing it in the donate pile. Every once in a while, we went through each other's closets to see what we could donate, sell, or trade. We'd never had much money growing up, so actually having extra clothes was a big deal to us. But we also remembered going through donation boxes and racks at thrift stores to find items that we could actually wear for school. So, we made sure we donated as much as possible. We weren't the same people we had been when we were younger. I had a steady job, one that I literally put my blood, sweat, and tears into. Jennifer was a stay-at-home mom for now, but anyone who's ever known or been a mom knows that there's nothing *stay-at-home* when it comes to being a mother. Jennifer was constantly on the go with her daughters. But when they got older, she wanted to go back into the workforce. But that was up to her and her husband. I would support her no matter what she did.

"You didn't sleep with him?" I blurted, not realizing that the question had been in the back of my mind this whole time.

"No. But you have. I saw the way you're walking all bow-legged."

I threw a throw pillow at her. "You're a bitch."

"Well, yeah. But he's clearly making you happy. And

that makes me happy. Because you need it. And I'm not just talking about dick. Although, you needed a dick, and now you've got a dick. And you're getting all the happy."

"You're very lucky your baby girls are out with your husband right now. You don't want them walking in on their momma talking about dick."

"But good dick. And let me tell you, my husband gives good dick. And from that cat-in-cream smile on your face, Devin gives you good dick, too."

"You're so weird. I'm not talking about that."

"Fine. Give me no details. I see how it is. But, seriously, I'm glad that he makes you smile."

"We're just friends."

"Friends who bone. And don't give me that shit. You talk about him. He's part of your life. You're not *just* friends."

I looked down at my hands, fisting them in front of me. "We are. We've already laid out the rules. We're in our nice, firm, little box, and we're not going to step out of it. I'm not ready for a serious relationship."

"Well, what about Devin? Is he ready?"

I shook my head and then froze. No. He couldn't be. He just wanted this to be fun for now, too. When he was ready to move on, we would both move on. And no one would get hurt.

"Everything's fine, Jenn."

"I know you say that, but I'm worried about you. If you

keep telling yourself it's just friends with benefits or whatever title you're using, things implode. They roll into one thing or another, and if you're not open to that, you're going to get hurt."

"No, I'm going to get hurt if I don't set those boundaries. I'm fine. I'm having fun. So is he. And it's good to just let loose once in a while."

"And yet you're letting him help you with work?"

I shook my head. "Maybe. But that's because we're friends first."

She studied my face. I didn't know what she saw there, but she turned away and looked back in her closet. "Okay. I love you. And I trust you. I just don't want you to get hurt."

I sighed and then got up so I could wrap my arms around her from behind. I leaned my head against her back and blew out a breath. "I don't want to get hurt either. That's why I'm being careful."

"You can be careful all you want, but sometimes, you can't help it. You know what we grew up with."

And that was the perfect segue into why I was over there for the day. I just hoped she didn't hate me for it. Considering we were already at odds when it came to Devin and me, this would probably end badly.

"I have something to tell you," I said, wincing when she stiffened.

"Well, that change in subject doesn't bode well."

She turned in my hold and pulled away, folding her arms over her chest.

She'd piled her hair on the top of her head, and she didn't wear a stitch of makeup. I knew she worked hard on her skin and had a nice, wide array of skincare products that I tried to pilfer every once in a while. She was gorgeous, happy, and living her best life.

I really didn't want to ruin it.

But I was missing something. And I needed to find it.

I just hoped that I didn't break us both in the end.

"I hired someone."

"Well, considering we were just talking about you getting Devin's dick, I guess you didn't hire a gigolo."

That made me smile. "No. But I did hire someone to find Dad."

Her eyes widened, and then she shook her head, her jaw tightening.

Our dad left us when we were young. And our mom had worked so many jobs trying to keep our heads afloat that she had lost part of herself. I remembered going hungry, I remembered smiling and laughing like it was Christmas when we actually had a whole can of tuna for dinner.

I remembered living out of our car for one semester of school, and the looks the other parents gave my mom. Looks of pity and scorn, as if it were my mother's fault that she only had a high school education. Our dad had been the one

171

providing for us, and then he skipped town with all of our savings.

He had taken Mom's identification, even our birth certificates.

And it had cost money to get those things back. Money we didn't have. We lived on government sponsorships and programs. But that money had dried up quickly. Even through all of that, we'd had a roof over our heads. Sure, the roof had been a car roof for a semester, but other than that, we always had running water and a place to sleep.

We had been safe, at least as much as we could be.

And we knew our mother loved us.

But she was always distant. Jennifer and I had grown closer over those years, even with our age gap.

And then, as soon as she could, our mother left us. I wasn't even old enough to be called an adult yet when she left. But Jennifer had been able to take care of me, and Mom had run off to a commune. One where she could just be free and the woman she needed to be.

I hadn't known that type of woman was inside her the entire time. One who could leave us just so she could find herself and be who she needed to be.

As an adult, I understood that you needed *me* time, had to be able to find moments to just breathe, and figure out who you were.

But we were her children. Her responsibility. And as

soon as she had been able to hoist that responsibility off onto someone else, she'd left. Just like Dad had.

But at least I knew where my mom was. I didn't know where my dad was. And I needed to know. I just needed to know.

"You hired someone," Jennifer said, her voice dull.

"I need to know where he is, Jenn. Need to know what happened. Why he didn't come back."

"Because he's a deadbeat father. That's why he didn't come back."

"Maybe. But I need to know."

I kept repeating it, and Jennifer kept pulling away.

"Good for you. But I'm done. He left us, Erin. Left us with our crazy mom."

"Mom isn't crazy," I said, rationalizing it like I always did. Yes, she was irresponsible now, but she had been responsible during our childhood. She'd kept us fed and clothed. That had to count for something.

"You know, maybe Mom isn't crazy. But she's living in a commune with a group of people we don't know because she was done dealing with life after raising us." Jennifer shook her head and pushed past me to fold a pile of clothes she had made. I tried to help, but she flicked her hand, pushing me away. "I have my family," she said, continuing. "I have my life. I don't need Dad."

I looked down at my hands, and then at her, wondering why what I had wasn't enough for me. Why it had never been enough. "I don't have that. I guess I just need to see. Let me have this." I didn't know why I needed her to be okay with my decision. Why I had thought that maybe she'd want to come with me if I ever got a chance to see him.

But she wasn't going to. She wanted nothing to do with it or with him. And I hated myself a little for how badly I wanted to know more. To know *him*.

"And when you get hurt, you know what you can do?" Jennifer rolled on me, and I took a step back, pain radiating through my heart and down my arms. I didn't want her to hate me. I didn't want her to push me away like everyone else had.

Because everyone did.

Just like Devin would eventually.

"What? What happens when I get hurt?" I asked, my voice hollow.

"Fuck," Jennifer muttered. "I won't say I won't be there. That I won't be by your side. Because I'm always going to be. I'm your big sister, damn it. I will always be here for you. But I can't see him. I can't talk to him. I hope you understand that."

"I do. It's my decision."

"Okay. So, just don't get hurt. Because you don't deserve that. None of us do."

And then she opened her arms, and I curled into my big sister. Our lives hadn't been perfect, far from it. But we always had each other.

She was the one person I knew I could rely on, no matter what happened.

That was a lesson I had learned young. One I had brought with me.

I'd tried to lean on Nicholas, attempted to make my marriage work. And I failed.

I wasn't going to do it again.

TWELVE

DEVIN

———

THERE WAS A TIM MCGRAW SONG THAT HAD COME
out when I was like a freshman in high school or so, and it
flashed in my mind as soon as I saw Erin slide into my truck.
It was like we were in Texas, and there were cowboys and
ranches and horses around. I swore I could hear the familiar
twang, and even though it wasn't Labor Day weekend, and I
wasn't seventeen, I could just see that song as she came up to
me in that miniskirt. And, yes, I was indeed wearing a white
T-shirt. One that, according to her, was tight enough to
showcase the muscles in my arms, and the ink sliding down
my sleeves.

Not too bad.

But that damn miniskirt? Yeah, she was killing me in it.

She also had that suntan line and had put on red lipstick to go with her jean miniskirt and red tank.

There were probably a few other country songs that I would be singing by the end of the day considering that we were on our way to an outdoor country music festival over at Red Rocks. But, seriously, Erin in that skirt was going to be the death of me.

"Devin, if you keep looking at me like that, you're going to have to pull over so we can get each other off before we go to the festival," she said, tugging down her skirt.

I groaned, gripping the steering wheel harder. "Seriously. You've got to stop talking like that."

"You're the one who started it."

"You're the one wearing that skirt."

"Really?" she said, and I looked over, wincing.

"You know I didn't mean it like that."

"Oh, I know. And I am wearing this skirt to get you hard. And because I'm hot."

"Yeah, damn straight, you're hot."

"I meant, it's hot out. We're going to be outside. And the amount of sunscreen I'm wearing is a little ridiculous right now."

"Well, you just let me know when you need me to apply some more."

"You're a lecher."

"But I'm your lecher."

She gave me a weird look and then shook her head.

"What?"

"My sister said something similar, but about her being my asshole."

I chuckled, turning into the parking lot. "Do I want to know?"

"Nope. It was a few days ago, and not that important."

I had a feeling from the tone of her voice that it was very important, but I didn't press her on it. She didn't seem to want to talk about it, and we were about to meet the rest of my family and our mutual friends. Not the best time to get into it.

"Well, I'm here if you need me."

"I know." She studied my face, and the heat between us died just a little. I wanted to know what she was looking at, what she was thinking. But, again, not the right time.

"Okay, so how did we get time off for this?" she asked, unbuckling her seatbelt.

I quickly got out of the truck and walked over to her side to help her out. She slid down my body again, and I held back a groan.

"We really need to get you a stool or something."

"You know, one time I was in a grocery store and this big truck—I think it was a dually even—pulled up in front of the entrance. The passenger side opened, and this stool was thrust out on a rope."

"A stool on a rope?"

"Yep. And then she used the rope to position the stool exactly where she wanted it and then got out and then put the stool back in."

"You don't need a damn rope. If I was going to actually let you get a stool, then I would get my ass out of the cab, walk around, get the stool, and help you down."

"Ah, but what if the man couldn't?"

"Well, that's one thing. But I am not going to let you have a stool on a rope." This was a ridiculous conversation, but it was making her smile. Me, too.

"Anyway, it's my normal day off, and you were able to actually take some time off for yourself, and everyone else sort of just worked it out. My friend Tucker is the one that got us all the tickets, so we were able to make it all work. Only Dimitri and Thea aren't coming up because they have something going on today with Thea's family."

"The infamous Montgomerys."

"Infamous is a good word for them."

"You know, now you're making me a little worried about meeting them."

"Oh, you've probably met one or four. They're Montgomerys. They're just everywhere."

She shook her head and laughed and reached for her purse. She slid it over her body, and I tried not to look how it pressed her boobs apart ever so slightly. I really needed to calm down. We had a long day of being near family and in close proximity to others ahead of us. I really didn't need a hard-on the entire time.

"Okay, so who's going to be here?" she asked, sliding her hand into mine.

"Well, Caleb is coming."

"Really?"

"Yep. He's actually gracing us with his presence."

"You said he hadn't been to a couple of your family dinners recently."

"Not the last two. But it was mostly for work. We don't let him sulk for long."

"Do you know why he's sulky?" she asked.

"Nope. We'll figure it out. I think Dimitri and I are the first wave, and if we can't figure it out, Amelia can."

"Aw, that's kind of nice that you save her for last."

"Nice? She's dangerous. We save her for last because we don't want her to come after us."

"That's so sweet for your little sister."

"You say sweet, I say she's evil. But she'll be here. And so will Tobey."

"Are they dating?" she asked as we handed over our tickets. They took her bag to search inside it, and then we walked through the metal detectors.

"Not that I know of. But she wouldn't tell me if they were. But they're chummy and nice and snugly. I don't really know. And I don't *want* to know. If he hurts her, I'll castrate him. That's pretty much all I need to know."

The guy walking near us winced and then gave me a tight nod.

Either that man had younger sisters and understood, or he had daughters. Either way, he got it.

"I don't think you need to castrate him. I think Amelia can handle that on her own." Erin grinned, and I shook my head.

"You know, that's true. Oh, by the way, Zoey will be here. And Tucker, of course."

"How have I not met Tucker yet? I thought he was one of your best friends."

"He is. He just works a lot. He's a diagnostic radiologist?"

"Are you asking me?" she asked with a laugh.

"No, but I always forget exactly what it's called. All I know is that he's fucking brilliant and works longer hours than we do. And Zoey's coming because she's friends with all of us, and it's nice to see her around."

"It is nice to see her around. She's been a good friend."

"And so it will be the group of us. I'm just glad you're here."

"Aw, that's nice." She went on her tiptoes and kissed me, her lips soft against mine. When her mouth opened, I deepened the kiss, and then groaned against her lips when someone cleared their throat.

"Really?" Caleb asked with a growl. "You've been here

for like two seconds, and you're already making out? Is this what type of day we're in for?"

"Oh, be nice, they're all sweet and in love and happy," Amelia said, leaning into Tobey. I looked up and raised a brow. I met her gaze, and she winced, blushing.

We were not going to discuss the *L* word. No way. After all, Erin wanted nothing to do with that, right?

"Well, I for one am glad you're here," Tucker said as he pushed past Amelia, winking down at her. He had physically pushed her, so she flipped him off. He just ignored her.

My best friend leaned over, took Erin's hand, and brought it to his lips. He was very lucky that I didn't kick him in the balls right then.

"Ah, even more beautiful than I remember."

"Remember?" Erin asked, confused.

"Well, Devin speaks about you so much, I have a clear vision of you in my head. Plus, there was a photo."

She turned her head to me so fast, I held up both hands.

"Of your face. We didn't take any of *those* photos. Dear God, Tucker. You want to get me killed?"

"And you wouldn't be showing off naked photos of Erin," Caleb said, looking all serious. "At least, not without showing me first."

"Okay, now I'm going to have to kick your ass, too," Erin said, acting sweet as sin.

It was Caleb's turn to hold up both hands.

"You know, I think she could do it," Caleb said, meeting my gaze.

"Yeah, she could," I agreed.

"*She* is standing right here. So, you must be Tucker. It's very nice to meet you. Even if that was a very strange introduction."

Tucker just grinned that patented smile that made women go to their knees in effigy and drop their panties. And a few men for that matter.

I still didn't know why I let him be around Erin.

"It is wonderful to meet you. It's nice to see the girl who has my guy over there all twisted up."

"Shut it," I warned.

"Yeah, I don't think I do that," Erin said, looking at me with an easy grace.

There was nothing easy when it came to what I felt for Erin. But that was my problem, not hers. We were going to have fun today, goddammit.

"So, who's playing today?" Zoey asked as she walked up to Caleb.

I looked between the two of them and held back a wince.

Caleb, honest to God, didn't even notice her. Well, he noticed her presence, but not Zoey herself.

I vaguely remembered Zoey pining over him back when we were in school. But that had been years ago. Apparently, the crush hadn't ended.

And Caleb was just as oblivious as ever.

Well, there went my baby brother, annoying the hell out of me just by not noticing the wonderful woman beside him.

Although, honestly, I didn't know if I wanted Zoey to have to deal with my brother.

"So, who's playing today?" Tobey asked, echoing Zoey's earlier question as he put away his phone. "I didn't really have time to look at any of the headliners or lists. But Amelia said she wanted to come out, so I'm here." He grinned down at my sister and kissed the bridge of her nose.

She blushed, and I met Caleb's gaze, and then Erin's, and then Zoey's, and then Tucker's.

We all just shook our heads.

Were they dating?

Well...maybe.

But if I asked, Amelia would likely kick me in the shin, and I really didn't want to have to deal with any new bruising.

"A few local bands are starting soon, and then the bigger bands will wrap it up. It's an all-day thing, though, so do you want to go get a couple of beers and maybe some food?" Amelia asked, pulling out her phone but still leaning into Tobey.

"Beer sounds good," Caleb said.

"A beer sounds wonderful," Erin said as she wrapped her arm around my waist.

"I should have tried to bring Jenn and her husband. They never get to do anything like this."

"Kids?" Tucker asked, staring down at her with such intensity that it worried me. But that was just Tucker. He was an intense kind of guy.

"Yes. Three little girls."

"I can probably scrounge up three more tickets if needed."

"No, it's fine. They have plans as a family. But maybe next time we all do something like this."

"I think Jenn would like that."

Tucker snapped his fingers. "Jenn. Your ex?" Tucker waggled his brows, and I flipped him off.

"Hey, I'm fine with it. And you get to be, too," Erin said sweetly. But I had a feeling there was a bit of edge to that. I liked it.

"Hey, I'm not getting in the middle of that."

Zoey left Caleb's side and wrapped her arm around Tucker's waist. Tucker slid his arm around her shoulders and kissed the top of her head.

"You like to get in the middle of everything, Tucker," Zoey said with a laugh.

"She knows me. It hurts. But she knows me." He put his hand over his heart and gave his chest a good rub. "Okay, I already know where we're sitting, and I got it set up for us. VIP seating and everything."

"How did you get all of this?" I asked, narrowing my eyes.

"It pays to know people."

"It pays to sleep with people," Caleb muttered and ducked Tucker's fist.

"Hey, I didn't sleep with anyone. I just charmed, smiled, but it was all out of the good of my heart. No sex was needed."

"Apparently, he's just that good," Zoey said, and the women tittered.

I met Caleb's gaze and then Tobey's, and then just shook my head.

I really did not want to have this conversation in front of my baby sister. Call me old fashioned.

We settled down in our seats, each with a couple of beers, a whole lot of water, and I got to feel up Erin's back and neck when I redid her sunscreen.

She narrowed her eyes at me over her shoulder when I did so, but it was totally worth it.

The music was good, the company was great, and it was just a good time.

It was nice to hang out and simply enjoy myself.

I worked hard, but I loved my job. I was outside most of the day, so I already had a good tan going, even over my tattoos, which wasn't the best thing. But it couldn't be helped with my job.

I slathered up with sunscreen as well and made sure that

everyone else did the same. Maybe Dimitri was right, and I was a mother hen.

I didn't mind.

Someone had to do it.

By the time we were all ready to head out, I was a little exhausted and probably overheated, but relaxed.

It had been a good day, and being with Erin like this? It made me feel like there could be something more.

I was probably setting myself up to fail, but I didn't care. I liked her. I enjoyed being with her.

I didn't like the idea that I was her rebound, but maybe something could come of that.

Not all rebounds were bad. Sometimes, you still made the shot.

We said goodbye, and I helped her up into the truck, my hands sliding under her skirt ever so slightly when I did.

She raised her brows, and I grinned.

"You want to go park somewhere?" I asked, my voice low and growly.

"I think if we don't, I'll probably try to give you a blowjob as we drive, and we might end up in an accident. I don't want to hurt your truck."

I didn't think I'd ever run around the truck as quickly as I did then. Soon, we were on our way to the quarry we had been to before, knowing we'd be safe. Anywhere else? I wouldn't have done it. But...desperate times and all that.

I had my hand on her leg, slowly stroking up and down,

getting closer and closer to the edge of her skirt with each passing caress. When my pinky scraped along the bottom hem, she sucked in a breath, and I did my best to keep my eyes on the road. I squeezed the steering wheel and then slowly slid my hand under her skirt, rubbing my finger along her soft skin.

I swallowed hard, taking the turn probably a little too quickly, but we were safe. I wouldn't hurt her.

But, goddammit, I needed to be inside of her.

I brushed my fingers along her heat, finding the lace panties she wore soaking wet.

"Dear God," I bit out.

"Are we almost there?" she asked, panting.

"We'd better be because I'm almost there myself."

She chuckled harshly and then gasped as I rubbed her clit through her panties.

She arched for me, rotating her hips with my touch. I did my best not to kill us both as I parked.

And then our seatbelts were off, and I was tugging on her panties.

Her lips were on mine, my mouth crushing hers, our tongues tangling.

I couldn't breathe, couldn't focus. I just needed to be inside her.

I reached inside my pocket, pulled out a condom, and then worked myself out of my jeans.

She helped me along, making sure she was completely

out of her panties. And when I pulled the seat back and patted my lap, she grinned at me.

"We'll make it work this time."

"But damn, that miniskirt."

"I've been singing that Tim McGraw song in my head all day," she said as she slowly worked her way over the center console.

"Yeah, me, too. You know there's one part where he says he has to work so hard for that first kiss. What do you think, you going to make me work hard?"

"Hey, as long as you're hard, I don't care."

"Dude." I started to laugh.

"I know. That was bad. But I really can't wait anymore."

I sheathed myself in the condom, gripped her hips, and slowly slid her over my length.

We both gasped, her warm cunt squeezing my dick hard.

I tugged on her tank top, and then on her bra until her tits popped out, then I leaned forward and sucked each one into my mouth. I bit down and worked at her nipples until they were pebbled and red like cherries.

"You're so fucking sexy."

I slid my hands down her arms, slowly sliding my hips just enough so I worked in and out of her.

She rocked on me, her mouth parted as she met my gaze.

Her skirt was rucked up over her hips, her shirt tangled

down right above it, and her bra askew as her tits bounced as she rode me.

I was still in all of my clothes, my pants just a little pushed down so my dick could be out and inside her.

I'd never had sex in this truck before. The only other time I'd been close had been when the two of us had gotten each other off.

This was probably the sexiest thing I'd ever seen.

She put one hand on the roof of the cab, the other on the back of my seat, and I gripped her hips with one hand as I used my other to palm her breast.

She worked me, bouncing up and down on my dick as I thrust inside her.

And when I used my hand to slide from breast to breast over her clothes and then moved to her clit, she came, clamping around my dick so tightly that I almost filled her immediately.

I kept going, though, slamming in and out of her, using the floor of the footwell to get the most of any thrust I could.

She kept going, too, her whole body flushed, and then I came, hard, fast. And she came around me again, her mouth on mine, neither of us looking at each other, just feeling.

I couldn't breathe, couldn't do anything except want to be with her.

She was mine in this moment, and if I let myself think hard about it, she could be mine forever.

But as the orgasm waned, and we cooled, and our breaths started to slow, I noticed that the windows of the truck had steamed. But we didn't care.

This had to be it for now. I had to be okay with this.

But as she looked at me, I saw something there in her face, an emotion I couldn't name. Something I wanted to name.

Maybe this *could* be more.

I really hoped it could be.

THIRTEEN

ERIN

———

I WAS APPARENTLY REALLY GOOD AT MAKING RASH
decisions. Recently, anyway.

No, that wasn't the case. At least, I tried not to make it
the case.

But I had told myself when Nicholas and I ended that I
would figure out who I was. And in order to do that, I had
to discover where I came from.

That meant I needed to figure out where Dad had gone.

Jenn knew my plans, and while she didn't support
them, she supported me. If this went horribly, which it
probably would, I knew I could go to her.

But I didn't want to. I wanted things to be okay. I wanted them to work out so I wouldn't be stressed out. I wanted my dad to hold me and tell me that he loved me. I wanted there to be some excuse for him having left us like he did.

Like the FBI or aliens or something.

At least, that's what I'd wanted when I was a little girl.

I wasn't a child now. I'd had those blinders ripped off long ago. Even before our mother decided that she didn't want to be a mom anymore and joined the commune.

It was just Jenn and me now. We were a family. And then she had made her own, and I had thought to make a family with Nicholas.

Somehow, I had been left alone, left behind. Again.

And that was why I needed to try and be okay on my own. Why I needed to be okay with this new version of Erin.

But it wasn't easy when I was so worried about what might happen next.

But that was fine, I would be fine.

I was going to find out why my father didn't want me. Why he left.

I was going to uncover the answers.

The detective I'd hired had found my dad.

I still couldn't believe it.

I looked down at the note in my hand. Frank Rose.

He lived less than an hour away, up in Fort Collins.

He still lived in the damn state.

Our mother didn't even live in Colorado anymore.

She had moved to Wyoming. Sure, just a state north, but she didn't live *here*. My father, the one who had abandoned us first, lived closer.

And he hadn't thought to contact us.

I'd imagined at one point that maybe he had gone to prison or something. Or perhaps he had disappeared and lost our phone number and forgot where he once lived.

Anything would have been easier in my heart and mind than knowing that he had left us but didn't actually move away.

But I had to be okay.

Because if I weren't, that meant that all of this would be for nothing.

And this?

What was *this*?

I was sitting in my car at a gas station, halfway between my home and the place where Frank Rose apparently lived.

I'd known about his address for four days. And I hadn't done anything about it.

I hadn't told Jenn. I hadn't told Devin.

What would I tell them?

Devin knew about my family. He knew because he had known us when we were younger. He knew that my dad had left us. And he knew now that my mother had left just the same. In fact, she had left soon after Devin and Jenn broke up.

Maybe I should have told Devin about finding my dad. But I hadn't.

And that was on me.

I was such a mess.

I didn't want to have to rely on him. Because once I did, things would get serious too fast. And if I let it be serious, then I would think about what those feelings were deep inside of me. And I didn't want those. Not really. I'd had them before, and they had broken me.

I just wanted this to be fun. Why couldn't I just let things be fun and not serious and just make things work?

Why did I always have to make things hard?

But here I was, sitting at a gas station, looking down at the address of the man who had raised me for what...a minute?

The man who had left us.

I needed to know why.

And I couldn't let it break me.

Because if I let it get to me, I didn't know who I would be after the fact.

I'd worked so hard to figure out who this new Erin was. The one without Nicholas by my side. Would I be a strong woman that could handle anything?

Apparently, not. I'd had to rely on people when my

place flooded. I hadn't been able to handle it on my own. And, yes, a small part of me realized that asking for help was a very big part of learning how to be strong and independent.

But I didn't want to. I didn't want to let anyone in.

Because people hurt you. They broke you.

I wiped away the tears that fell down my cheeks and cursed at myself.

Here I was, overthinking things again. I was just going to look at the house. I wasn't going to call. I wasn't going to look him up. I was just going to see. And then I would go home and figure out what to do next.

Because I was scared—so damn scared.

And I didn't like being afraid.

"Okay, Erin. Time to put on your big-girl panties and just get it over with. It's going to be fine. Everything is going to be fine."

I gave myself a nod in the rearview mirror, started my car, and pulled out of the parking lot.

The drive was easy. It wasn't rush hour, and I-25 was in decent shape in this area. If I had to go south, I probably wouldn't be as happy, but I liked this part of the drive.

I'd been to Fort Collins countless times. I hadn't known that Frank Rose lived here.

He had even kept his name.

He hadn't gone under some secret identity or done any

of the things my imagination had supplied when I was younger.

No, he had just left us. Moved away. But maybe it was for a reason.

Maybe he just didn't want children. Perhaps he didn't want any of that. Maybe he wanted a completely new life.

One without us.

I shook my head and followed the GPS off the highway and into a newly developed neighborhood.

My stomach clenched as I looked around. I swallowed hard.

This wasn't some downtown urban area. This wasn't going to be a shelter where some down on his luck old man now lived.

No, there were children playing basketball on driveways. Others in yards, playing jump rope and other games.

Little kids on bicycles with helmets and elbow pads and even knee pads.

There were parents all around, constantly watching. Hovering.

This was a neighborhood that took care of its children and watched them.

This was a place for families.

My hands shook as I took a turn down another street with identical houses and smiling people.

"Why are you here, Dad?"

I didn't mean to whisper the words. I didn't want to say them at all.

They just poured out of me.

This wasn't a place for a man in hiding. This was a place for a man who was living.

I took another turn, and my GPS told me I had arrived.

I parked in front of the neighborhood playground and turned off my engine, but I didn't look to the left.

I didn't look where I knew the house was.

Because if I did, then I would be there for real. And everything would be different.

This couldn't be happening. I couldn't be in such a family-friendly neighborhood.

Maybe it was a mistake. Perhaps this was a different Frank Rose.

Of course, the detective had been a hundred percent sure that this was where my father had ended up.

How long?

Not too long, considering the ages of the homes here.

But, dear God. What did this mean?

I finally gathered the courage to look left, my heart in my throat, and my stomach aching.

It was a perfect two-story home with blue shutters and white trim. It looked as if it had been power-washed recently because there didn't seem to be a speck of dirt on it. There was a large porch with a hanging swing and a screen door that had glass on it that looked as if it let in the sunlight when they wanted to open the wooden door.

There was a paved driveway and a walkway through the yard.

There was even a white picket fence.

I didn't even know they made white picket fences for front yards anymore.

Most homes only had back fences. Hardly ever white. And certainly never with actual pickets.

But this whole neighborhood had white picket fences around the lots. Not on every one, but enough of them that it seemed to be part of the HOA.

My father lived in a perfect house, with perfect paint, a perfect yard, and a perfect little white picket fence.

Maybe he was just visiting.

Maybe this wasn't his home.

Maybe he hadn't left his family for this.

Maybe he hadn't left *me* for this.

This had to be wrong. This wasn't where he lived. I rechecked the address and shook my head. Maybe the private detective got it wrong.

Well, I could sit here and stare, or I could go see.

Maybe I would just see.

The PI hadn't told me anything else. I hadn't asked him to dig deeper. He'd just said that he found Dad and offered to look more into it so I would know what I was walking into.

But I hadn't wanted to know. It wasn't about the money, I just didn't want to know.

But now I was facing it, head-on, and I had to take the next steps. I had to figure it out.

So, I pulled my purse strap over my head and got out of the car, my hands shaking.

I locked the doors and looked both ways before I crossed the street, then smiled at a little girl on her bike as she waved. Her hand went right back to the handlebars as her mom chased after her with laughter in her voice.

The little training wheels on each side of the back wheel shook ever so slightly. I couldn't help but wonder what would have happened if I'd had kids like my sister.

Would I be that mom?

I hoped I would be.

My mom had tried, but then she hadn't been enough for us. We hadn't been enough for her. But Jenn had been there for me.

My Dad hadn't.

He had been somewhere else all this time. And now, he was here.

I unlatched the gate, walked through, and closed it behind me.

No one really paid much attention to me. All of their eyes were on their own things, their minds on their own worries. But I knew they saw me. I knew they saw a woman in jeans and a top with boots, her blond hair braided behind her head.

I looked normal—hopefully not like a serial killer or a salesperson.

I didn't know what I wanted them to see. I could only focus on taking each step in front of me. One, and then the next.

Before I could take my next breath, I was there. The door was firmly closed as my finger pressed the doorbell.

I was doing this. I was going to see my dad. This was okay. He would just tell me what happened, and everything would be all right. I wasn't going to freak out.

The door opened, and a boy of about fourteen with sandy blond hair and a crooked smile looked at me. He was lanky, probably tall for his age, and just learning how to use those long limbs of his.

But I wasn't really looking at any of that in real detail. No, I was looking at his eyes.

Because those eyes, the shape of them, the color...those were *my* eyes.

What were my eyes doing on a fourteen-year-old boy?

Or fifteen, or sixteen. A teenage boy?

I couldn't breathe, I couldn't do anything. I was looking at someone who had to be related to me. And this was Frank Rose's house, at least according to the detective.

Horror washed over me. I knew exactly who this was. This was Frank Rose's son. A son that he'd had with another woman. One he'd kept while he hadn't kept Jennifer and me.

"Hey, you okay? You look a little pale. Do you want some water?"

The boy spoke quickly, his voice at that stage in puberty where it was just starting to crack, just starting to get a little deep.

He was a teenager.

He had to be my brother.

Right? Or maybe I was just seeing things. Imagining things in order to make sense of it. Maybe he wasn't related to me at all. Maybe those eyes were just common.

But Jenn's babies had those eyes, too. And so did my dad.

"Who are you talking to, son?" a deep voice asked from the living room behind the kid. My hands shook, and I clenched them at my sides. "Is it Jessie from next door?" Frank Rose asked as he took a few steps forward.

He put his large hand on his son's shoulder, gave it a squeeze, and then looked up. His eyes widened ever so slightly, and I wondered what he saw?

Did he see the little girl he had left behind?

No, I didn't think so. He wouldn't know what I looked like now. He wouldn't remember the little girl he had left far too young. He wouldn't remember the child he had shattered in so many ways. The one that had learned to rely on him, only to learn to depend on no one.

Because they all left. Everybody left you broken in the end.

I looked like my mother, though. Other than my eyes and maybe a few gentle slopes of my face, I looked exactly like my mom. Is that what he saw right then? I didn't know, but he looked at me, an older version of the man I had seen in photos. The father I could barely remember. He knew who I was.

"Hey, Con. Why don't you go in the back and help your mother, okay? I have to take care of this."

"Are you okay, Dad? She looks like she needs some water or something. It looks like she saw a ghost. You think we have ghosts?" Con asked, turning into his father's hold like he didn't have a care in the world. Like his dad loved him with everything that he had, and nothing was ever wrong or missing in his life.

Why did this kid have that while I didn't?

Why did it hurt so much?

"Don't worry about it. I'll handle it. You go help your mother."

"No problem, Dad. Nice to meet you, lady."

He waved at me and then ran off to the back where his mother presumably was. A mother that he had in his life, the woman Frank Rose had stayed with.

"Jenn?" Frank Rose asked, his voice low.

And that was enough for me.

He thought I was my sister.

Because he had done the math and figured it couldn't be his wife. The one he left. No, it had to be his daughter. But he'd been wrong. I wasn't Jenn.

"Wrong daughter, Frank."

I couldn't believe I could actually speak just then, but nothing else came out. He blinked again. I didn't know if he was going to say or do anything else. So I turned around and walked away as quickly as I could. I wasn't going to run. I wasn't going to scream and shout and ask him why he left us.

Because I didn't have that in me.

He had created the perfect family, the ultimate life. My family—my mother, my sister, and I—hadn't been enough.

That was clear as day.

I made it to my car, and he still didn't say anything. I got in, set my purse on the passenger seat, turned on the engine, and pulled away.

I got as far as the Community Center part of the neighborhood before I pulled over, my body shaking.

I couldn't breathe. I couldn't do anything.

He hadn't said anything. Hadn't even looked at me.

My head hurt, and so did my heart. Because I knew I needed to get home, I needed to be safe, I picked up my phone and called without thinking. Because I knew he would come for me. At least, for now. Until everything changed.

"Hey, babe, what's up?" Devin said, his voice so soothing, I didn't want him to hang up. Because what happened when he walked away? Who would I be then?

"I need you," I said softly. Breaking my rules. The ones that had kept me safe for so long. No, that was a lie. I wasn't really that safe, was I?

"Where are you?"

I told him, and he said he'd be right there for me. Though it was probably going to take an hour since I wasn't anywhere near home.

I just sat there and looked at my hands, wondering how it had come to this.

How could I rely on someone else?

I couldn't do this. I couldn't depend on anyone but myself. I couldn't get hurt again. Because if I fell for this man, if I fell for Devin, I'd always be worried. Worried whether I could pick myself back up again if things fell apart.

I had fallen once, then had been left by my father.

Fallen again, then left by Nicholas.

I wasn't sure I could do it with Devin.

I wasn't sure I could remain whole if he left me.

I wasn't sure I could remain whole at all.

I was afraid. So afraid that if I let myself love him, there wouldn't be anything left of me when he left.

Because they always left.

That was the one thing I knew.

They always left me behind.

I needed to push Devin away before he hurt me. It was the only way. Even if it broke me. Because I couldn't hurt him either. I couldn't let him fall and end up broken.

I cared about him too much for that.

So, I'd have to do it first.

I'd have to be the one who ran.

And I'd probably hate myself for it.

Every. Damn. Day.

Fourteen

DEVIN

I HAD WOKEN UP THIS MORNING WITH ERIN IN MY arms, both of us fully dressed, and her nuzzled into my chest, my chin on the top of her head.

I had never been so scared as when I got her call the night before.

She had said that she needed me. And I had wanted to break something for her, needed to fix it all. But I couldn't. There was nothing I could do for her except hold her. But she had come to me. Or at least, she had asked for me. That meant something. She had asked me for help, and I had gone to her.

When I arrived, she had been sitting stoically in her car, looking down at her hands, not doing anything else. Her face had been dry, but I had been able to see the tear tracks down her cheeks.

She just looked at me, her eyes wide. Something had changed. Something was different.

I wasn't exactly sure what, but hopefully I would find out later today.

She had told me why she was in Fort Collins. And I'd wanted to rip something in half. I'd wanted to growl as I stormed into that jackass's house to demand an explanation.

But she hadn't wanted one. She'd emphatically said as much. And I didn't want to hurt her by forcing one out of the man who was supposed to be her father.

My dad hadn't been the greatest, but at least he hadn't been like that.

Yeah, Dad drank a lot. A whole hell of a lot. But he hadn't left us. Until he died.

Yes, Mom had cheated on Dad, but she hadn't truly left us either, until she died, too.

No, our parents weren't perfect, but at least they hadn't moved to a new community in the same fucking state to start a new family.

Erin had told me the whole story without really blinking, seemingly without feeling.

I hadn't known what to do, so I'd called Caleb to come

and pick up her car, just like I had when she first walked back into my life in that sequined dress of hers.

Both times, she hadn't wanted to show that she was hurting, so she had hidden inside of herself. And, both times, I did my best to just be there for her.

Caleb had brought her car back to my place and hadn't asked any questions. But I knew he would be there for me.

Just like I knew that Jenn would have been there for Erin if she had asked for help.

But she had stated firmly that she did not want to bother her sister.

So, I'd just held her all night, listened to her, but she hadn't cried. She hadn't done much of anything.

She had been sort of wooden, but that was okay.

Because she would get through this. And I would be by her side.

Yeah, we were friends with benefits or whatever the fuck you wanted to call it, but we were something else now, too. We had to be something else. Given the way she leaned on me?

Things were going to be okay. Yes, she was in pain. No, I couldn't fix it for her. But I could be there for her.

Things would be okay.

Erin was at work today, apparently finishing up cakes for three weddings all at once. I wasn't a hundred percent sure how she could do all of that, but she was good on her feet, and damn good at her job.

The fact that I knew I probably needed to start working out a little bit more so I could fit into my jeans after trying out all of her cakes meant that I really wanted to keep her.

After all, Dimitri had had to do the same thing when he got with Thea. Apparently, it was part of a Carr's life to fall for a baker.

I blinked and looked down at my phone. Had I fallen for her?

Did I really love her?

I liked being with her. I enjoyed her in my life. I was starting to plan things around her. I thought about her all the time. And if she wasn't sleeping at my house, I was staying at hers.

I had a feeling we were way past the friends with benefits stage and had moved into full-blown relationship status, even if she didn't want to use the title.

But did I love her?

I think I did.

And that...yeah. Yeah, that scared me. But that was fine. I would be fine.

And so would she.

As soon as she figured out exactly what she thought and felt about me.

That was a little scary. But I wasn't going to think about that. We would just keep going slowly. And I would gradually show her what she meant to me. And then, maybe, just maybe, she would trust me.

Because, damn, I really needed that trust.

And I really wanted her to love me back.

But I didn't have time to worry about that right then. I'd figure it out eventually. I always did. I wasn't going to let this pass me by because I was worrying. At least, I hoped I wouldn't.

I stuck my phone into my back pocket and went to the bed of my truck where I'd put a few flower boxes that Amelia had asked me to pick up. She had a vehicle of her own, but since it was my day off, I'd said I would help out.

Her job was gaining business, even as we headed into her least busy season of the year. She would need to hire new people soon, but for now, Caleb, Tobey, and I were helping out. I'd even gotten my friend Tucker to help out a few times, but with his job, he rarely had time to help. Dimitri helped when he could, of course, but since he was an hour away, it was easier for those of us closer to help out.

I didn't think Dimitri would ever move to Denver again, not with his woman and her family down in Colorado Springs. I had known that for a while now, but it was just starting to sink in as my brother began to settle in with his family, and I was looking to do the same. This was how things were going to be from now on.

It didn't really bother me all that much since it wasn't like we were a plane ride away or anything, but all of us had figured out our places and roles in this family of ours, and mine was apparently the mother hen.

Who knew?

"Hey, you brought them, thanks!" Amelia said as she made her way to the back of my truck. "And you set them on blankets so you wouldn't hurt your baby."

I eyed her. "Of course, I did. This truck is worth far more than your flower boxes."

"That is true. I can't believe you even let us dare ride in it." She put her hand over her heart and fluttered her eyelashes. "I mean, I almost have the vapors, Devin."

"I'm going to beat you," I grumbled, holding in my laughter.

"I'd have to take you out," Tobey said, coming around Amelia. "Let me help you out, babe." He reached across her, and my little sister froze, staring at the other man as he lifted the boxes.

Babe?

Since when did Tobey call my precious baby sister, *babe*? I'd have to talk to Caleb and Dimitri about this.

As Tobey walked off, Amelia must have guessed where my thoughts had gone from the look on my face. "Shut up."

"Hey, I didn't say anything." I carefully reached in to take out the blankets and then shook them before I folded them and put them back into the truck.

"You didn't need to."

I shook my head and leaned down to kiss the top of her head. "You're imagining things," I lied.

"Gaslighter."

I winced. "Okay, fine. Sorry. I'll do better about not wanting to punch any guy in the face who looks at you weird or calls you *babe*."

She nodded her head primly. "That's all I ask."

"You don't ask for much."

"Oh. I do. Sometimes. But, anyway, thanks for bringing these around. Are you coming over tonight to watch the game?"

I nodded. "That's the plan."

"Bring your girl with you." She grinned and walked away, and I just shook my head, smiling right back at her. "My girl," I whispered to myself. I liked that.

In fact, I should go visit Erin. I had things to do today because I didn't really get that many days off, but the time that I did have, I liked to be near her. I would just see what she needed, see if she was doing okay. I knew she was probably busy, but maybe I'd try to help. She didn't accept assistance easily, but you never knew, perhaps I could get her to let me pitch in.

She had seemed sad that morning, had pulled away a bit. I figured it was about her dad, so I was going to figure out how to help.

Because I loved her.

Jesus Christ. I loved her.

And I needed to make sure that I got to keep her.

She was running around the kitchen when I walked in, her hair falling out of her bun, and things moving a mile a minute.

I immediately went to the sink, washed my hands, and looked down at her.

"Hey, let me help."

She looked at me, her eyes wide. "Oh. You're here. I thought I was going to see you later. I'm fine, Devin. I don't need your help."

"Your staff isn't here." I looked around and frowned. "Just let me help."

"You shouldn't be back here. You're not on my staff, and you're not covered under my insurance."

My brows rose. "That didn't really stop me before."

"Because I was stupid, okay? I really don't have time for this. You should go. I've got this. I have this all handled."

"Yeah, you do. But you don't have to do it on your own."

"You don't get it, do you?"

I frowned, shaking my head. "I don't think I do at all."

"Okay," she said, letting out her breath. "You know what? I was going to do this later, but I can't."

I froze, blinking. "It's over. It was fun while it lasted, but it can't continue. I just need some space." She said the words so quickly, I didn't really comprehend them. It was like they weren't actually coming from her mouth. Like it wasn't really her.

What the ever-loving fuck?

Rage spilled out of me, and I tried to hold it back. I

knew this likely had something to do with her dad, must have something to do with what had gone on in Fort Collins, but I was pissed. So fucking pissed. "What's next? It's not you, it's me?"

"Hey, you know what? It's a saying for a reason. We've had our time. But now it's time to move on. We're friends, right? Let's just do that. I need some space."

"With another man?" I growled out the words and then froze. How the hell did that come from my head? "You know what, I didn't mean to say that. It's not what I meant."

She paled just a bit, but then her eyebrows lowered, and her nostrils flared. "You know what? Sure. That can be a reason. But just go, Devin. Thank you for your help. For everything." She swallowed hard, and her eyes went glassy, but she blinked the tears away so quickly that I almost missed it. "Thank you for everything," she repeated. "But this just got too serious, too quickly, and I wasn't looking for this. I don't want to hurt you. So you just need to go. Okay?"

The mixer turned on the counter behind her, something beeped on the oven, and her phone started ringing. And all I could do was stare at her.

She was pushing me away.

Pushing me away, and I didn't know how to fight it.

I didn't want to force her to love me.

Didn't want to make her do anything.

She didn't want to hurt me?

"Too late, Erin. Too. Fucking. Late."

Her eyes widened. I didn't care. I couldn't. Because I didn't know how to fix this. I was the one who was supposed to be able to fix things, right? And I couldn't.

She didn't want me. Fine. I wouldn't be here.

I just had to figure it out.

I turned on my heel, and I left. She didn't call me back.

She didn't reach out for me, didn't want me to come back so we could talk it out.

She had said right from the beginning that this had to be casual.

I had been the one to change that.

So, fuck it.

Apparently, it was over.

For good.

Fuck.

FIFTEEN

ERIN

I MEAN, I KNEW I WAS AN IDIOT. I KNEW I HAD
things to work through. I knew I needed to protect myself. I
knew I needed to protect Devin.

But, apparently, I was a bigger idiot and more of a
horrible person than I ever knew.

"I miss you, Heath," I said, whispering at my TV as I ate
my cookie dough right out of the jar. They made edible
cookie dough these days, perfect to help me when I was a
stupid idiot who didn't know how to talk about my feelings
and tell anyone what I was thinking. Not that I actually
knew what I was feeling or thinking.

But edible cookie dough could at least help. Maybe.

That and watching *10 Things I Hate About You*.

When Heath Ledger died, I had done my best to never watch another movie with him in it. It physically hurt to see him. It hadn't been like that with other actors. I had quickly been able to fall into a Robin Williams movie or even an Alan Rickman film. It had hurt to watch them, but maybe it was because I knew what the loss of Heath Ledger had done to me that I had thrown myself into watching *Sense and Sensibility* or *Die Hard*. Into watching *Aladdin* and *Patch Adams*. Of course, the latter probably wasn't the best idea for me because it just made me cry harder. But I had watched those movies. However, in the years since losing Heath Ledger, I hadn't watched a single one of his films. I owned all of them on DVD, Blu-Ray, and digital. Mostly because I hadn't wanted my inability to watch him to hurt the bottom line. Not that it actually mattered in the end, but my brain was weird that way.

But today, I'd decided it would be the perfect day to watch the first movie where I had fallen in love with him. When Patrick sang that beautiful song to Kat with the marching band, I loved him. When he smiled, those dimples peeking out from his face, I had fallen for him hard.

It didn't seem fair that he died so young.

So now, I was weeping into my edible cookie dough, worried about him rather than my own life. And that was good. Because I was allowed to be sad about Heath. I couldn't be sad about my own decisions. Because I had been the one to make them.

I had been the one who made those mistakes.

So, if I was feeling poorly or wanting to throw myself off a bridge or something because I was that stupid, it was my own fault. And that was just something I would have to live with.

I was an idiot.

Patrick said something to Kat when they were on those swings, and I just closed my eyes, trying not to think of Devin.

I didn't know if I wanted to get to the end of the movie where Kat tells him all the things she hates about him. But mostly the thing that she hates about herself.

Because that was me.

I hated myself so much.

I'd been so worried about getting hurt, that I had hurt the person who mattered the most.

And it wasn't until I was actually saying the words to him, being callous and cruel, trying to push him away, that I realized how much I cared about him.

Now, I couldn't take that back. I couldn't magically make everything better and heal him.

He didn't deserve that.

He deserved someone that wouldn't lash out when they got scared. He deserved happiness.

And I definitely wasn't that.

The scene cut to Joseph Gordon-Levitt, and I paused the film, not knowing if I wanted to continue the movie. Plus, I was a little nauseous from all the cookie dough I had eaten.

They said it was completely edible and egg-free, and I had yet to get salmonella from any type of cookie dough, but maybe this would be my lot in life.

I was a baker, after all. Dying by baked goods and bad decisions seemed like the perfect thing to be written on my tombstone.

My doorbell rang. I sniffed and looked over my shoulder.

It wouldn't be Devin. He wouldn't be here. He wouldn't come to me, trying to get me to work it out, or even just to get me to speak with him.

He hadn't called, hadn't texted. And I hadn't reached out either. His last words to me were that I had hurt him. I deserved the pain I felt.

Because I was stupid.

I sat my cookie dough down next to my glass of wine, the one I hadn't really touched because I didn't want to get drunk again.

I'd had too many drinks when I found out that Nicholas was cheating on me.

And thinking about that just made me think of Devin, so I hadn't even taken a sip of my wine.

It felt weird to waste a good glass, but it just wasn't in me.

Nothing was anymore.

I opened the door. Zoey stood there, a bit of pity in her eyes, but also some anger.

I deserved that, though, didn't I?

I was a horrible person.

"Hey. You look like shit," Zoey said as she pushed past me into the house.

I closed the door and wiped the crumbs off my T-shirt and sweatpants.

I had put my hair on the top of my head, and I was pretty sure I had cookie dough stains on my shirt, as well, but it didn't matter.

I needed to wallow in my misery. Because I was the one who had done this.

Not Devin. Devin had been amazing. No. I was the evil one.

I deserved to look like crap and feel like crap.

Because I was crap.

"I know why you're here, but you can't make me feel any worse than I already do."

"Babe, I love you. But you're a mess." Zoey picked up the cookie dough, looked at it, raised her brows, and then went over to the fridge to put it away. She also tossed my glass of warm wine and put away the bottle that I had left on the table.

"You don't have to clean up after me."

"No, but I will. Because I love you. And Amelia would be here, too. Because she's a friend, but things are weird."

"That's what happens when you date your friend's brother. Things get weird. You don't have to be here either. I know you're close with the family. And you and Caleb—"

She cut me off with a look that could cut steel, and I winced.

"Sorry."

"It's fine. I'm friends with Caleb. Nothing more. It's something that we all know. But I am your friend. And Devin has everyone else, so you get me." She winced. "Well, that sounded worse than I meant it to sound."

"No, it sounded just about right."

"Okay, sit down and tell me what happened. Because I want to know why you pushed him away."

"Well, what do you know?"

I sat down on the couch opposite her and just looked down at my hands.

"Amelia and I were at her shop when Devin came storming in, saying he needed to dig something or beat something up with his hands. We didn't know what it all meant, but Amelia asked how you were doing because that seemed like the thing that might make him act like that other than his work and maybe a dog. And he just said that things were over. That you had ended it. That he was fine.

Just fucking fine." She sighed. "His words. A total lie, by the way."

"I'm an idiot."

"You keep using that word, and you're probably going to keep telling yourself that. But unless you do something about it, you're worse than an idiot. However, I'm not going to yell."

"You're yelling a little bit."

"Because I love you. But just tell me. What happened?"

I looked down at my hands again, wishing I could have my cookie dough. Or cry. Or do anything but face the poor decisions I'd made and continued to make.

Zoey looked at me, shook her head, and then turned off the TV so I couldn't finish watching *10 Things I Hate About You*.

Well, there were more than ten things I hated about myself right then.

And, pity party of one, Erin speaking.

"I went to see my dad."

Zoey's eyes widened. "You found him?"

I nodded.

"You didn't tell me. You didn't tell any of us, Erin. Why didn't you?"

"I told Jenn. She didn't want to go. She said that she was done with that part of her life. She said that he left us, and she wanted nothing to do with it or him. But I had to know.

I had to know why. Well, it was wrong. I made a mistake. Something I'm apparently good at."

"Oh, God, what happened?"

"I went there. He lives in Fort Collins."

"You're serious."

"Yep. He was there, presumably with his wife since he mentioned her being at the house in passing. And he has at least one son. A teenager named Con. I think he's around fourteen. And he loves his dad. He was polite, sweet, and he wanted to know why the nice lady on the porch was acting so funny. And Frank Rose put his hand on Con's shoulder, gave it a squeeze, and called him *son*. And said that his mom needed him in the back. So, yeah, my dad, my deadbeat father, who didn't want us and ran away, has a happy family. With a white picket fence. A fucking white picket fence. How does that even exist? I thought that was only in the fifties."

"They're starting to make a comeback in some developments. But that's really not the important thing. Oh my God, I'm so sorry, babe."

"Yeah, I am, too. I shouldn't have gone. I should have just let myself continue thinking that he was in witness protection or in jail or dead. Something that wasn't him having a perfect life that had nothing to do with the first family he'd forgotten. I've become a statistic, Zoey. A fucking statistic. And I got so weird about it that I couldn't even drive home. So, I called Devin to come and get me."

Zoey's eyes widened. "And he came. Just like that. No questions, no explanations?"

"He didn't need any. He came right to me and made sure I was safe. And then he held me all night. I didn't cry but thought I would. Thought I could. We even kept our clothes on. No sex. We were only supposed to be friends who had sex. I wasn't supposed to rely on him. Want him. Need him as much as I did."

"Did?"

"Do? It doesn't matter, does it? I ruined it. I ruined it because I was scared. And I can see it. I could see the wrong decisions that I made in my head as if I were an outsider. And I just wanted to shake myself. But I couldn't, and I can't go back. You can't go back when you hurt someone like that."

"You didn't cheat. There're other ways you can go back. He'll forgive you."

"I don't deserve it. I told him that it was nice, and that we were done. And then he asked me point blank if it was for another man. I knew it was just a slip of the tongue because he got stressed out, he even apologized after he said it, but for some reason, I figured that, sure...why not tell him that? It'd be easier to let him walk away. Not get hurt. But it was stupid. And it makes no damn sense. So, yeah, he walked away after telling me that I hurt him and that he was done. So, I guess it's over. Because I'm stupid."

"Babe. You're not stupid. You just made some stupid decisions. But you kind of are a fool."

My eyes widened, and I blinked away the tears. "A fool. I'm not stupid, but I'm a fool?"

"Well, I didn't like you constantly putting yourself down just then. But you really are a fool."

"Thank you. This is helping."

"Oh, shut up. Devin's so good for you. And you're good for him. I don't know why you had it in your head that it had to be short-term and just for fun. Devin's worth more than that, and so are you."

"I had long-term, and Nicholas spat on it. Actually, he fucked the head cheerleader while doing coke off her chest. I'm pretty sure I'm done with trying to be full-time. And being in a real relationship. I wasn't very good at it. I couldn't keep Nicholas."

"No. You didn't. But that's on Nicholas. Not you. He's an asshole. He always wanted more, and he used you to get it. That's just the way it was. It wasn't only him doing that woman in the bathroom. He always treated you like a second-class citizen. But you were getting better. You were finding yourself and becoming independent."

"So much for being independent. I kept having to rely on everyone else just to get things done."

"In emergencies, and because we love you. Being independent means you don't have to rely on somebody, but you can. Or something like that. I don't know. All I know is that you have good friends that love you. So, we're going to be there for you. Just like you would be there for us. Just like you have been there for us. I don't like that you can't see that. Do you understand that when things are going wonky at my store, you come right over and help? That when Mrs. Murphy needs something, you're right there. You just don't see that, and I hate that for you. And as for Devin? Just because you weren't looking for something, doesn't mean it wasn't supposed to be there. You need to fix this. Talk to him."

"I don't know what to say."

"Start with you're sorry. And tell him what you feel."

"I don't know what I feel. I've been telling myself for so long that I shouldn't feel anything when it comes to him, that I just can't figure it out."

"Then do so. Figure out exactly what he means to you. That way, when you talk to him, you don't hurt each other more. Because he's great for you. Just like you're great for him. But get it done. Fix this. Okay? I want to see you guys live happily ever after and have all the amazing love and happiness and sex and all the stuff that you enjoy."

"Did you just say you want to watch me having sex?" I asked with a laugh, still shaking a bit.

"Well, I'm not really good with the words. But I want you to have a life that you deserve. And don't tell me you deserve anything less than pure happiness. Because you deserve everything. You're my best friend. And Amelia is too, but she's not here at the moment, so I'm just going to call you it."

That made me laugh. "I'm really not good at this sort of thing."

"I know. I'm probably worse at it than you are. But you have a chance to fix it. So, do so."

"I could love him, Zoey. I think if I let myself. I could really love him."

"I know. So, wallow a bit more tonight. We're going to finish this movie, even though it makes me cry just thinking about it."

"I know. Same."

"And then you're going to shower, wipe off whatever cookie dough you have smeared all over yourself, and stop looking like the bedraggled old mess that you are."

"You're such a good friend. Honest. But good."

"I'm sure you'd do the same for me. Not that I'll ever actually let myself get to this point, but I digress."

I gave her a look, and she shook her head.

No, tonight was not about Zoey and her decisions. Tonight was all about me.

And, yes, I needed to fix this.

And I would.

Because I could love Devin.

If I let myself. I just had to figure out how to do that.

SIXTEEN

DEVIN

TODAY SUCKED. BUT THEN AGAIN, MOST DAYS THIS week had.

I did my best not to look the dog in the eye as I finished up my route. But it kept stalking me, its little claws tapping on the pavement behind me.

Seriously. I did not have a problem with dogs. I loved them. Mostly. But I did not like the dogs on my route.

The beast yipped at me, its little high-pitched bark grating my ears. And then it growled, still high-pitched, with just a slightly deeper tone to it. I finished up the mail for the day, closed the community mailbox, and then turned to look at the dog. I didn't need this today.

It kept barking, coming closer to me with each hop, and then backing away. One hop forward. Bark. Back away. Hop forward. Yip. Back away.

"Okay, buddy. Where's your mama?" I asked. I knew that the dog lived two doors down with a single woman who enjoyed coming out to get the mail from me personally. She always made sure that her tank top was pushed just a little lower so I could get an eyeful of her ample bosom.

Yes, I used the word bosom. Because that's what it felt like. Like I was meat on a stick, and she wanted to rub herself all over me. And, of course, she always brought the dog.

That thing had tried to bite me at least six times since I started this route.

One that was coveted by others at my station, and yet no one really wanted to deal with this particular canine. It wasn't mean, not really. It just had that little dog personality where it needed to protect its territory even though it was itty-bitty.

I couldn't reach down and pick it up because I didn't want to get in trouble for kidnapping a dog. Nor did I want to get bit.

However, I couldn't really move either. Because if I did, it followed me, yapping. If I tried to get closer to the truck, I was afraid it would go under a wheel or something or run out into the middle of the street and get hit.

Dear God. I was exhausted.

I hadn't been sleeping. I was no longer used to sleeping alone. And didn't that just piss me the fuck off?

"Seriously, where's your mama? Why aren't you on your leash, or in your little basket? Or in her arms?"

Miss Mahan loved this little dog, and she never let it out of her sight. She pampered the little thing and constantly went to get it pedicures, not just clips, but actual pedicures. I didn't judge. As long as she was happy and the dog was happy and not biting me, I didn't care.

But the dog was getting really close to biting me. Really close.

"Okay, Pippy. That's enough." I tried to put a growl into my voice, so I sounded more authoritative, but Pippy just kept yipping.

"You need some help, Mr. Postman?" a man asked as he rolled by on his bike. He didn't even look back, and I really wanted to flip him off. But I was in uniform. So, I couldn't. I also couldn't punch the man or try to get rid of the dog. No, I just needed to get back into my truck and go home. Well, back to the office anyway. And then home. I really just needed to get away from this dog. And I didn't want to think about why I was having such a bad day.

Because that all had to do with a certain somebody who'd told me to get lost.

And, apparently, I was single now. Single and pissed off.

Because Erin didn't want us. She didn't want me. She wanted to do everything on her own, and wanted nothing to do with me.

But that was fine. I could do everything on my own, too. Like, get rid of this dog.

"Okay, Pippy. Go back to your mom, please."

I sighed and went to the back of my truck to finish setting everything up.

"Stop following me, Pippy." The dog kept barking, yipping.

This would be how my life ended. With a dog yapping in my ear. It would forever haunt my dreams. Yip yip yip, bark bark bark.

All because of a tiny, little dog named Pippy.

It was a Pomchi, a Pomeranian/Chihuahua mix—or so her mama had told me—with bright pink bows in its fur, and hot pink claws.

The dog was usually pretty happy about life, but right now, it hated me.

Well, that was just great. I was the mailman. I suppose dogs were supposed to hate me.

Maybe it was the shorts.

Honestly, I wasn't a fan of the shorts.

"Where's your mama?" I asked again as the dog barked.

I didn't know if Pippy would follow me if I kept moving towards the house or end up in the street.

And with its sharp little teeth, I wasn't really sure I wanted to deal with bending down and trying to pick it up.

I was not about to get bit by a dog. No, thank you.

Miss Mahan still hadn't come out of her house, so I had a feeling she didn't know Pippy was out on her own.

Well, that was just great.

However, before I could figure out exactly what to do, Pippy decided to take matters into her own hands. Paws? She came at me, barking and trying to claw at me, I moved to the side and cursed under my breath.

She rolled out into the street and kept going, right into the middle of the double-lane road. I swore every ounce of blood moved away from my face.

"Fuck."

I ran out to get her, trying to be faster than my legs actually allowed. I might be in shape. I might work out and run and be on my feet for hours a day.

But I couldn't outrun a car.

I reached down for her, but it was too late.

There was a skid of brakes, a loud screech, and as I pushed the dog out of the way of the oncoming vehicle, she bit me gently on the hand, but that didn't hurt.

No, the car hitting me in the hip hurt.

There was a flash of light, a scream, and shouts.

But I didn't hear much of it.

No, all I could do was feel the blinding pain on my hip,

the gravel along my face and my side, and everything else
that came from getting hit by a car.

But the dog?

The dog kept yapping.

So at least Pippy was fine.

Me, on the other hand?

Ouch.

And then, there was nothing. Only darkness.

Seventeen

Erin

BAKING HELPED RELIEVE STRESS. AT LEAST THAT'S
what the experts said. And while I loved baking and *loved*
my job. Baking *for* my job when I was already stressed out
about what to do with Devin didn't really help things.

I wasn't truly stressed. Not really. Things were going
okay at work. The place was back up and running. The roof
had been fixed, the flooding damage was gone, and insurance had paid for almost all of it.

I had a healthy savings account, mostly because I tried
not to do anything that revolved around a social life, other

than things with Devin recently, so I had the money to fix what the insurance didn't cover.

So, work was good.

It was just everything else that wasn't great.

After Zoey had left the night before, both of us a little blotchy, and our eyes swollen from watching *10 Things I Hate About You* and remembering our dear Heath, I had taken a shower like she asked me to. Something I desperately needed to do. And then I had gone to sleep, knowing I would have to find Devin today and go down to my knees to say I was sorry.

Only I felt like I needed to find a different way to do that.

Not that I *wouldn't* go down to my knees, and not in a dirty way like my mind kept supplying.

No, I needed to find a way to prove to him that I wasn't scared. Well, I *was* scared. That was the problem. I was scared that he would leave me. I was scared that I would get hurt.

But acting like I had with him, hurting him and therefore myself in the process, hadn't worked out.

I had to find trust. I just needed to realize that he was going to be there for me. Because he wanted to.

Because he had never done anything to make me think that he wouldn't.

My lack of trust was all on me.

And that sucked.

I had just finished putting the last of my cakes in the fridge for the next day so I could go through my tablet and figure out what I needed to do overnight while I was thinking, when my phone rang.

I looked down at the readout and picked up.

"Hey, Zoey."

"I'm on my way to pick you up. We need to go to the hospital. Devin's been hurt."

Everything froze inside of me. It was like time stood still. I could actually hear the tick-tock of the clock on the wall. I could hear the building groaning and settling. I heard the wind outside.

I could hear my heartbeat slow. It wasn't going fast, it wasn't speeding up as if I were in danger.

No, it was as if everything needed to slow down so I could figure out exactly what Zoey had said.

"Hospital?"

"I don't know all of it. But he got hit by a car while working."

My hands shook, and I tried to look around for my purse, my keys, anything.

I needed to change out of my work shoes. I needed to do something.

Oh my God. "He's alive?" Bile coated my tongue, and my hands shook again.

"He is."

There was a screech of tires out front, and then Zoey was running into the shop.

"I left the car running, and I'm double-parked. Come on. Get your stuff. I'm getting you to the hospital."

"He's okay?"

"I don't know. He got hit by a car, Erin. Amelia just said I needed to get there."

I froze.

"*You* needed to get there."

"Yeah. So, let's go."

"His family's not going to want me there. Devin won't want me there. Just let me know if he's okay. I just need him to be okay. He can't be hurt."

What was he thinking, getting hit by a car like that?

"It makes no sense. He's usually so careful."

"I think there was a dog involved."

"But he pretends he hates dogs. Why would he do that?"

"I don't know. We'll get more answers at the hospital. You're coming with me."

"He's not going to want me there."

"Well, tough shit. You're going. See? This is one way you can make amends. You can go there and be by the love of your life's side while he's hurting."

"Okay. But if they don't want me there?"

"Then fuck them. They're my friends, too. I love them. But you need to be there. Okay?"

I nodded, knowing she was right, even though I was scared. But fuck this. I had been scared before, and I had hurt Devin. I wasn't going to hurt him again. No, I was going to fix this thing between us. But first, he needed to be okay.

Hit by a car?

How could that happen?

He had to be okay. I couldn't lose him just as I found him. Right when I'd already let him slide through my fingers once.

I would do anything to make sure he was okay. Even never see him again if that's what I needed to do. Just that thought made me want to break down and cry. But it was fine. He would be okay. He had to be okay.

I grabbed my purse, quickly shut everything down, and locked the door behind me as I ran to Zoey's car.

I slid into the passenger seat and let her drive. She was a pretty calm driver, and I didn't think I would be able to do it in her place.

"He's going to be fine, Erin."

I looked over at Zoey as she pulled into the emergency room parking lot, and I nodded, wiping the flour and sugar from my pants.

"Yes. He's fine. Everything's okay. I just...he has to be okay."

"He will be."

"I'm sure."

I walked like a robot, just going through the motions as I followed Zoey into the ER.

People waited in groups, some coughing, some just sitting there, listening for their name to be called. Zoey kept going, her eyes on her phone as she texted with somebody. I assumed it was Amelia because she seemed to know where she was going. We went down the hallway to another waiting room. This one was a little more private. And everyone was there.

Amelia and Caleb were standing and talking with Tobey pacing nearby. He came and put his arm around his best friend.

Tucker was also in the room, pacing in a corner.

Dimitri and Thea were there, as well, both of them holding each other as they spoke to Caleb.

Everyone was there.

The family had been called. And I hadn't.

But what did I expect?

I had dumped Devin. I had been a bitch.

They didn't need to tell me anything.

After all, I was nothing to them.

Amelia looked up at me, her eyes widening for a second, and then she turned her back on me. She leaned into Tobey, and he rubbed his hand down her back. Caleb just glared, and then started to pace on the opposite side of the room from Tucker.

The two of them didn't talk to each other, and nobody really paid attention to me.

But then Zoey rushed into Thea's arms, and the two held each other. And I was left standing there alone.

Because I was an idiot.

Because I had been so scared about getting hurt that I had dumped him. What was I doing here?

The family didn't need me here. They had each other. They were all so close.

Devin didn't need me.

I was just about to turn away to go catch a cab or schedule an Uber, but then Dimitri was there, putting his hand on my shoulder.

I looked up at him, tears prickling the backs of my eyes. And then he hugged me. "Sometimes, we have to do what we have to in order to protect ourselves and then we realize later that we should have seen what was in front of us the whole time." He whispered the words, but I knew that everyone had heard.

People were looking at me. I didn't know what to say to them. How could I apologize for hurting their brother? For hurting Devin, especially now that he was even worse off.

I wasn't naïve enough to think that the world revolved around me and that he had gotten hurt because of me. At least, physically. Emotionally?

Yeah, I was that bitch.

"What happened?" I whispered.

"He went to save a dog from getting hit by a car and got hit himself," Amelia said, her voice icy.

Amelia needed someone to be angry at, and you couldn't be angry at a dog, so it seemed I was the target. That was fine. I deserved it.

"He's going to be fine, though," Dimitri said. "We just need to remember that." He rubbed my shoulder, and then Thea came closer and gave me a hug, too.

"As someone who's had to deal with hospital visits before with family members, it helps to pace and cry and just talk it out."

I wanted to ask her what she meant by that, but this wasn't the time or place. Dimitri and Thea shared a look, and I pulled away slightly, folding my arms over my chest.

Caleb was there then, putting his hands on my shoulders, and I looked up, wide-eyed.

"Fix this."

I blinked. "I'm not a doctor." And there was another stupid thing said.

"You know what I mean. Fix it."

"I want to. I just don't know how."

"You will," Amelia said from the other side of the room. "But he has to be okay first. That damn dog."

"You know it wasn't the dog's fault, babe," Tobey said, kissing the top of her head.

I just looked between them all and blinked away tears.

Devin had been hit by a car.

It didn't even seem real. We all stood there, taking our turns pacing or sitting down or just talking to one another. Most of them gave me space, but nobody really gave me the cold shoulder except for that instant when I first walked in. They needed a target to be angry at, and I was fine being that in the moment.

After all, I blamed myself more than they did.

It seemed like hours, but eventually, a man in scrubs walked through the double doors, looking exhausted but not defeated.

That had to count for something.

I stood frozen, so afraid to hear what he had to say. What we could lose.

Please be okay, Devin.

You have to be okay.

"I'm looking for the family of Devin Carr."

Dimitri cleared his throat and stepped forward. Thea's hand was in his, and the rest of the family moved closer. Tucker, Zoey, and I stood in the back, Tucker putting his arms around each of us as if we were our own little unit in the family of Carrs. Yes, Tobey was with Amelia, but that was fine. Everybody had someone.

Devin had to be okay.

"We're it. All of us."

The doctor nodded. "Your brother's a lucky man."

"He got hit by a car. How lucky can he be?" Amelia snapped.

"Babe," Tobey whispered.

"Sorry."

"No, you're right. I should have used a better word. He's going to be fine. He has a broken tibia and fibula on his left leg. But it was a clean break, so it should heal nicely. He's going to need some physical therapy for that eventually. He also lost his spleen from where he hit the pavement. That one's going to take a little bit longer to heal, but we were able to go in laparoscopically, so he should be on the mend soon. He's going to be in a boot for a while and will need to use a walker since he can't use crutches with the incisions. And then, after that, he can move to crutches. It all depends on how he heals and how much of himself he puts into it. But Mr. Carr is in good shape, physically fit. As long as he does what we ask him to do, he'll be fine. Now, who wants to see him first?"

The others started talking, and I backed away from Tucker's hold to sit down, my knees weak.

And that's when I let the tears come.

Devin was okay. He was going to be okay.

Why then did it feel like I was dying inside?

The tears came, and Tucker took the seat next to me, putting his arm around my shoulders as I cried into his neatly pressed shirt.

Devin was going to make it.

But I wasn't sure I would.

EIGHTEEN

DEVIN

DAY TWO OF STAYING IN THE HOSPITAL MEANT I knew I was a cranky asshole. But fuck it. I'd just had surgery, my leg was in a boot-cast thingy, and Miss Mahan had already been there with the damn dog to make sure I was okay. She'd been kicked out quickly for sneaking Pippy inside the hospital, but still.

I'd seen the dog I'd risked my life for, but I hadn't seen Erin.

Served me right for walking away like I had before and not trying. She'd been scared, and I'd pushed her away.

But, damn it, getting hit by a car should have brought her to me. Right?

Maybe she truly didn't want me. Well, hell, that sucked, didn't it? I guess it was well and truly over.

Good riddance.

"You're growling," Amelia said by my side, finally alone after Tobey had left to go clean up for work.

"Sorry." I mumbled out the word, and she just gave me a look.

Dimitri, Thea, Caleb, and Amelia were now in my room, staring at me.

Tucker had been in and out, so had Tobey. Zoey came as well with flower arrangements.

And yet, I still didn't see Erin.

"So, never do that again," Dimitri said after he'd cleared his throat.

I raised my brow. "Okay, I'll try not to let someone hit me with a car again," I growled out.

"Good," Dimitri barked.

This time, it was Caleb who laughed. "You know, I'm usually the grumpy asshole. Kind of looks like it's Dimitri this time. Also, how did all of us get back here? I thought they had a limit on how many people they let in a room at a time," Caleb asked, kind of looking around.

Amelia waved him off. "Thea and I handled it. Don't worry. We're not getting kicked out. Plus, we need to make sure that big brother here doesn't pop a stitch or something or be an idiot. Because, seriously, he got hit by a damn car."

"I didn't mean to. There was a dog."

"Are you sure you didn't throw the dog into the street?" Caleb asked, and I flipped him off.

"I don't hate dogs."

"And yet, one tried to kill you," Dimitri said, shrugging. "I'm just saying."

"The little thing came at me. I tried to get away from it, but it moved past me and into the street. When I tried to get to it, I got hit by the car instead. But the dog is fine."

"Yes, I saw the big busty blonde come in and make sure you were all good." Amelia kind of growled out the words, and I narrowed my eyes.

"Stop it."

"I'm just saying," she said, looking down at her phone.

I could hear the worry in her voice. All of them had been worried. Hell, *I* had been worried. I got hit by a car.

It was ridiculous.

"I'm okay," I whispered and reached out for her. I winced a bit, and she scrambled up from the chair to take my hand and close the distance. "Don't hurt yourself."

"Not any more than I already am, right?"

"You just need to get better, okay?"

"Yes. Because the fact that you made the news as *Postman Saves Dog and Gets Hit by a Car* or some shit like that is really too much for us. We're a nice, calm family."

I just glared at Caleb, and Dimitri shrugged.

"Well, we try to be calm. We're not always."

"Well," Thea began, "when you're out, we'll make sure you're all taken care of. We'll even have a little party or something. I can bring cheese. And, of course, cake."

Someone cleared their throat in the doorway, and I froze. I knew that voice. "I can bring cake, too," Erin whispered from the hall. Everyone moved out of the way.

Awkward didn't begin to cover it.

They all gave me guilty looks, and I had to wonder what the fuck that was about.

Soon, they left as if they suddenly had somewhere else to be, and I was left alone with Erin. The girl who had dumped me. And hadn't shown up until now.

Well, at least she had shown up.

The fact that I was still a bit full of sour grapes wasn't helping. I blamed it on the meds. I was just so fucking angry. Mad at myself. Upset at her. Pissed off at the damn car. No one had gotten in trouble. After all, I hadn't been too hurt. Spleen or no spleen. I would be fine. But I'd have to work behind a damn desk or something at work, which just angered me more.

I had worked for years to get the route that I wanted, and now I was going to lose it. And there was no promise that I would get it back once I could walk normally again. If I could walk without a limp at all. Jesus Christ, I had gotten hit by a car.

I looked at Erin, and I felt like I got hit all over again.

"I didn't mean for everybody to go," she whispered.

She had dark circles under her eyes, and her hair had been brushed back from her face in a messy bun behind her head. She had on her work uniform, but it looked like she hadn't slept at all.

Well, that made two of us. The only time I'd really slept was when I had been out of it and under anesthesia, and then on pain meds. None of that meant I'd rested. Not really.

"Well, apparently, they thought we needed some privacy," I growled out.

Yeah, now I was the asshole, but she had pushed me away. She had let me go. Why was she here?

"I came in yesterday with Zoey. But then they let Dimitri back, and I didn't come back today until I had some things handled. I just wanted to make sure you were okay." Tears slid down her cheeks, and I wanted to forgive her. I wanted her to tell me that she loved me and then I'd do the same with her. But I couldn't. She had pushed me away. Would she do it again?

She had said that she didn't want anything serious. Well, getting hit by a car was serious. Maybe this was just too much for her. Because it was certainly too damn much for me.

"I'm so sorry."

"That I got hurt?"

"Well, yes." She looked at her hands and moved forward. She stood right at the end of the bed. Still not touching me. But it was better. I honestly didn't know what I'd do if she touched me anyway. "I'm also sorry that I'm a horrible person. I didn't mean to hurt you."

I just looked at her. What did she want? Why was she here?

She wasn't professing her feelings to me. Only saying that she was sorry I'd gotten hurt.

Well, I was hurt. I was in a fucking hospital bed. And I couldn't even get up right then. They had pulled the catheter out of my dick at least, so that was something. But, Jesus Christ. I did not want to deal with this. I did not want to deal with anything. Everything that I had been working toward my entire life up until this moment was slipping through my fingers. And she was just standing there.

Literal evidence of what I couldn't have.

"Yeah, well, you did," I said, my voice harsher than I intended.

Her eyes widened, and she took a step back.

I didn't want to hurt her. But then again, it seemed this was what we were good at.

"You should go, Erin. Just go."

She opened her mouth to say something, but then she just shook her head and turned on her heel.

She left. She didn't want to stay. Didn't want to fight. Well, I didn't either.

I felt like shit. Hey...like I had gotten hit by a car.

Served me right.

Maybe I *was* the asshole here. Didn't matter, though.

I was going to lose the part of my job I loved, I had lost my damn spleen, and I'd lost the one person I thought I could love.

Seemed about right.

Just as I deserved.

NINETEEN

ERIN

———

"THIS FROSTING IS AMAZING," JENN SAID AS SHE dipped her finger into the bowl.

"I know. I made it." I smiled widely, but I knew it didn't reach my eyes. I also knew that Jenn knew.

I was fine. Seriously. It had been...what? Two weeks since I had walked out of Devin's hospital room. See? I was fine. I hadn't broken down or melted into a puddle. I hadn't been struck by lightning.

I was still standing. Apparently, making kick-ass frosting.

The fact that my sister was sitting in the customer area

of my little shop eating frosting out of a bowl I'd prepared especially for her meant that I was fine. No, my sister totally wasn't there trying to make sure I was okay. She wasn't checking up on me. Because there was no need to do that.

I wasn't a broken shell of the person I once was. Because I hadn't loved him, right?

I had pushed him away because I hadn't wanted to fall in love. I wasn't hurting right now. I couldn't be. Because if I were, that meant I had loved him.

I broke the wooden spoon against my counter and looked down at my hands.

"You okay over there?" Jenn asked, then she moaned. "Oh my God, is this actual vanilla bean?"

"I'm fine." I quickly cleaned up my mess, cursing myself. The spoon had been old and brittle anyway. Anyone could have broken it. Not just me. I was fine.

Maybe I should tattoo that right on my forehead. Or my ass. Because that's what I was. A big, fat ass.

"Do you need some time alone with your frosting? I mean, I can go walk into the back, and you can do whatever you need to."

"That's gross. But...maybe. Me alone with my frosting. Come here, big boy." She stuck her finger into her mouth and moaned.

"You're being gross," I said, laughing. It wasn't a real laugh, but it was warmer than my others. See? Progress. I couldn't wallow, I only had myself to blame.

"What?" she said, licking her finger.

"I gave you a spoon. If somebody walks in while you're doing that, I'll somehow end up in trouble with the health department or something.

"You can't. I'm in a place where people taste cakes. It's where I'm allowed to eat cake right off my fingers. Dear God, cake. And this is just the frosting."

"You really do have a love affair with frosting, don't you?"

"You're going to put this inside the cupcakes you're making me for my baby girls, right? Oh, yes, this inside the strawberry cupcakes with extra cream cheese frosting on top, mmm. I need some time alone."

"Yeah, maybe you do. And maybe I shouldn't be feeding that to your little girls if you're going to go off and orgasm over a bowl of frosting."

Of course, fate would let the door open at that moment, the little bell tinkling. I groaned.

Thankfully, it was just Zoey.

"Well, hey there, who's orgasming over frosting now?" she said, skipping in.

"Hey there, Zoey. It's me. And I would let you have some, but this frosting is mine. All mine. Mine, mine, mine," she sang as she ate more frosting. I just shook my head.

"You're going to get diabetes."

"No, I won't. You gave me such a minuscule amount of

frosting. I'm just going to take my time with it. Softly. Slowly. Achingly eating it bite by bite."

I met Zoey's gaze, and she just widened her eyes. "How long has she been alone with the frosting?" Zoey asked, keeping her voice casual.

"Not long enough," Jenn said, moaning.

I just laughed, shaking my head. "I think she's finally lost her mind."

"Maybe. But it's fine. Because all I need is this bowl of frosting."

"How many times do you think she's going to use that word today?" I asked, moving out of the way so Zoey could come back with her box of goodies for the wedding prep.

"Well, you do technically live in this bakery these days. So, probably a lot."

"I don't live here," I said, holding back my wince. Well, I sort of did. I'd worked more hours than I ever had before, not doing very good at the whole balance thing. What was the point?

Not only was I dealing with the fact that I would probably die alone, Nicholas had sent me a wedding invitation.

"So, did you answer yet?" Zoey asked. It was like she knew what I had been thinking about.

"No, I threw it away. I was going to circle no and say, 'fuck you,' on it, but I didn't want to come off as the bitter ex-wife."

"Still can't believe that bastard invited you." Jenn just

shook her head, coming over with the bowl. The one that was practically licked clean. No, there was nothing practical about it. My older sister, the one with grace and poise, the epitome of pure motherhood, had licked the damned bowl clean.

"I can't believe he did either."

"And you know what sucks? He didn't invite me."

I looked at Zoey and then looked over at Jenn.

"You're upset that my ex-husband, my *cheating* ex-husband didn't invite you to the wedding?"

"I was his sister-in-law for how many years? And he didn't invite me. But he invited you."

"I really don't know what I'm supposed to be thinking right now," I said, shaking my head.

"I'm thinking you should give me some more frosting," Jenn said, shaking her hips.

"Not even a little bit. You had enough sugar. Soon, you'll be bouncing around this place, and then you'll crash."

"Probably. But it's so much fun. I like pretending I don't have any worries and can just eat frosting. I'll probably be nauseated later."

"No, you won't. My frosting does not make you nauseous."

Jenn winced. "Well, maybe with the amount that I just ate."

"True, because no one in their right mind eats that

much frosting," Zoey said, ducking out of the way of Jenn's fist.

"I can't believe you were going to punch me." Zoey scrunched her nose.

"I was just going to do a love tap." Jenn shrugged and then went over to wash her hands.

"Anyway, Zoey, thank you for showing up to help with the last parts of the wedding. It's a big one tomorrow, and I want to get the final things ready. I need to actually be onsite for it because they want me to do the final cutting and everything after they get the photos done."

"Oh, I know it's a big wedding. I'll be there too, dealing with the flowers. And they even had Amelia there doing the landscaping because they wanted a pond with koi fish in it."

"Koi fish?" Jenn asked, coming in after she'd washed her hands. "They want fish at their wedding? And not just as an option for dinner?"

"I didn't ask. But there's probably a salmon dish."

"Well, that's just weird. It would be like having a steak option and having a cow next door." I just shook my head and laughed at my sister. I had been laughing more today than I had in a while.

But that was why Jenn was here.

Because she hadn't wanted me to be alone. After all, she had heard exactly what had happened with our dad. And after I had held her back from wanting to go and beat his ass, we had both decided that we weren't going to do anything about it. My dad, or Frank Rose as the bastard would now be called, hadn't even bothered to try and contact me. He hadn't reached out to my mother. Jenn had done the honorable thing and contacted our mom to see if Frank had called her. Nope, nothing.

He hadn't even bothered to confirm who I was or see why I had been there. But it was fine, everything was going to be just fine.

He had his perfect new life, and if our half-brother—something I didn't even want to think about, if that was really what he was to us—ever wanted to meet us, then we'd deal with it.

But neither of us, me or Jenn, were ready for that. Maybe one day. But for now? I had made the wrong decision by wanting to figure out exactly why our father had left us.

We hadn't been enough. Just like I hadn't been enough for Nicholas.

Maybe I would have been enough for Devin. If I hadn't run away when things got hard.

And that was enough of that.

"Devin's on crutches now," Zoey said and then froze in the process of putting flowers on the cake. Jenn cursed under her breath, and I just looked between them.

"Oh?"

"Thought you'd like to have an update. He's doing pretty good in the boot. The surgery went well enough that he practically has no pain. He healed up really quick. The bruises are gone, too. Well, he does have that thorn in his paw, but other than that, he's doing great."

"Thorn?"

"He's been a Grumpy Gus. Pretty much an asshole. But I don't know if that's because he's behind a desk now, the fact that he got hit by a car and therefore can't drive because he broke his leg, or because he misses you."

"I'm thinking it's a mix of all three. But probably mostly the latter," Jenn said, and I wanted to throttle them both.

"He told me to leave." I looked between them and rolled my shoulders back. "He said to leave, and I did. He hasn't contacted me since. Yes, I pushed him away first. So, I deserve this. It's over. I just need to get used to the fact that Devin is in all of our lives, at least on the periphery. I mean, I hadn't seen him for years before this, so it should be fine. I've worked with you and Amelia for years without knowing that Devin was close. So, I'll just work like I did before. Like it's not a big deal."

"That's not the best way to work on things sometimes, though, you know?" Jenn said softly.

"Well, it has to be the best for me. Because I don't want to hurt like this anymore. I don't want to feel this hollowness inside me anymore. I just want to do what I do best, and that's making cakes. Because that's what I'm good at."

Nothing else.

But I didn't say that.

I could have my own pity party in my head. They didn't need to hear it aloud. They had already heard enough. And yet they stood by my side, even when I was an idiot. So, I was going to try and be better for them.

Even if that meant that I never got to see Devin again.

Even if it broke me more each time I thought about it.

TWENTY

DEVIN

"I'M SURPRISED YOU DIDN'T SHAVE FOR THE wedding," Amelia said, coming up to my side. She patted my arm, careful not to touch me too much. They'd all been like that. Every single person in my family and all of my close friends. It was as if they were afraid I would break if they touched me. Well, considering that my body *had* hurt far too much before this, they were probably right.

I still ached something fierce. My incisions were pretty much healed at this point, at least as much as they were going to be until enough time had passed. I didn't have to use a walker anymore, and thank God for that. Having to watch my brothers figure out how to cut into tennis balls so they could put them on the bottom of the walker had been hilarious. But something I never wanted to witness again. Considering that we didn't have parents anymore, our next stage of seeing the elderly and doing things like that would be with each other. I really did not want to think about the progression of things like that. But the fact that they had all been there for me, no matter what, was pretty great. Caleb had slept on my couch, even though I had a guest room.

He had joked that he didn't want to bother me and had wanted to hang it over my head from now on that, yes, I had forced him to sleep on the couch.

My brother was an asshole. But he was pretty great.

He had moved out a couple of days ago, going back to his own place since it was new and all. But everybody did their best to stop by more often than usual.

Even Dimitri had shown up about every other day with Thea in tow.

Thea's family had even shown up at one point for a Montgomery dinner at my place.

The number of people that we crammed into my house was a little ridiculous, but they'd all wanted to make sure that I was okay. Then we'd all shared war stories about the times everybody had been in hospitals. Considering that there had been an actual gas explosion at one point, a mugging, and something else to do with a car, there were a lot of hospital visits.

I counted myself lucky. Yes, I had lost my spleen, but I hadn't lost my life. That had to count for something, right? Either way, my friends, family, and Thea's family all made sure that I was never alone.

Which, admittedly, kind of pissed me off. How was I supposed to brood and get all growly if I wasn't alone?

"Um, Devin? I asked why you haven't shaved. What's up, big brother?" I glared at my little sister, who wasn't even looking at me. She was probably looking for Tobey. They had come together, but Tobey had gone off to get her something to drink, and I hadn't seen him since. I was fine. I was just tired of people. The fact that I was at a wedding for a friend probably wasn't the best place for me. But I was here. In a suit. And a boot. On crutches. And, apparently, I had a beard that was annoying my sister.

"I didn't feel like shaving. I like the beard."

"Oh, I know you do. You even put a little oil in it so you look all nice and hipstery."

"First, hipstery isn't a word. Second, I was hipster before it was cool to be hipster."

"I'm pretty sure that's like *the* hipster saying."

I almost flipped her off, but that would have required me to let go of my crutch, and I wasn't in the mood to actually lean on my armpits again. Whoever invented crutches was a sadist. Dear God, I hated these things. I couldn't wait until I could actually put weight on my foot and leg again. The doctor said it would happen eventually, and at least I wasn't relegated to bed rest or some shit. Apparently, getting hit by a car ruined lives.

My life, anyway.

"So, when do you start back at work?" Amelia asked.

"Why'd you have to ask that?" Caleb asked, handing me a soda. I really wanted a beer. But because I might be on pain meds later, nobody would let me have one.

This is why I hate life.

Not the fact that Erin wasn't in it, or that I had pushed her away after she pushed me. But, whatever. I wasn't going to think about that or her. I could not think about her.

"What did I say?" Amelia asked, and then I looked at her. She winced under the weight of my glare, and I felt a little bad about it. A little.

"Don't mention the job."

I sighed at Caleb's voice. "I'm fine. I won't be behind the desk for long."

"You say that. But you're an old man now."

"Do you really want him to beat you up? I'm pretty sure he'd beat you up with that crutch."

I ignored my sister and just looked at my brother. "I'm thirty-four. I'm nowhere near retirement age. I'll be fine. I'll go back out on the road."

I might lose the route I wanted and earned, but I'd get it back. After all, I had gotten hurt on the job, and that meant something. Legal things were going on, and I'd find my way back to where I needed to be. I had to.

I really did not like being behind a desk. I liked being out. It was just the whole walking thing that was a problem right now. Hence the crutches. And the pain in my side.

"He'll be fine," Amelia said, giving us both a very regal nod. "I'm going to find Tobey. I don't know where he went."

I gave Caleb a look, but thankfully, neither of us said anything. Amelia was touchy when it came to Tobey. I just wanted to know what the hell was going on. But I wasn't going to get answers. Not from her, at least.

"The wedding was nice, though," Caleb said out of the blue, and I raised my brows.

"Yeah. It was pretty good. The grooms were happy. Both mothers of the grooms started weeping openly."

I grinned at that, and Caleb just shook his head, a smile playing on his lips. He took a sip of his beer and then looked out into the crowd.

"Yeah, they did. It's just weird that they would cry that hard at a wedding."

"Well, both of the grooms are the youngest of like six each, I think."

"Dear God, I thought four was bad."

"Don't let Amelia hear you say that. She'll kick you in the shin again."

"At least you have a broken one. That way, she can't kick you."

"For now. As soon as the cast comes off, I'm pretty sure she's going to go back to her kicking ways."

"That's our baby sister for you."

Caleb looked out on the dance floor again, his gaze enraptured by something or someone. I looked to see who it was but couldn't. I didn't know much about Caleb's personal life. After all, he'd been in and out of the state for a while. But he was home now. And the fact that somebody seemed to have caught his attention, well...I had to see who it was.

There had to be a hundred people on the dance floor, everyone shimmying and dancing and laughing and just having a good time.

But there was one person I recognized.

Interesting.

I wasn't going to say anything now. If I did, he'd bring Erin up, and I really wasn't in the mood to deal with that.

And now I really wanted a fucking beer. I hadn't had a pain pill all day, so I could have one. But my family wouldn't get me one. I'd just have to get one myself.

"I'm going to go find a seat. Probably inside."

"Okay." Caleb gruffed out the word, then shook his head, forcibly moving his gaze from the dance floor.

Very, very interesting.

I hobbled off to the kitchen, grateful that I was alone for a bit. I pulled a beer out of the bucket, nodded at the caterer, and kept going.

It wasn't easy to hobble on crutches with a beer in your hand, but I made it work.

Somewhat.

I walked into the kitchen and took a seat in one of the chairs, letting out an audible groan. That's when I noticed the cake.

There had been the main wedding cake out in the dance area, one that I knew they would be cutting soon, but this had to be the groom's cake. And it was gorgeous.

All chocolate with homemade-looking peanut butter cups and little race cars all over it. Perfect for one of the grooms.

The other cake was also a groom's cake, but that one had been a little more traditional—for the family, I figured.

That one had been all lace with black and deep red so it looked like crimson waterfalls running around and all over the levels. It was big enough to feed the five hundred people at the wedding, as well as whatever this groom's cake would be used for. Then I noticed that there was a bowl hanging on top of it, and I had to wonder what it was.

"Is that a bowl of chocolate?"

"Yes. It's a deconstructed swan. As soon as I put some liquor over it and catch it on fire, it'll melt on top of the rest of the cake, and then everyone can dig in."

I froze. I knew that voice. There were two people that I knew of who could make cakes as delicate and delicious as these. One was down in Colorado Springs and was related to me by marriage. The other?

She was the one I didn't want to see. Yet the woman that I wanted to be face-to-face with again no matter what happened.

I looked up, and Erin was there, her hands clasped in front of her, her face pale.

"I didn't know you were working here."

"Yeah. They asked me to be here to cut the cake for the wedding. It's actually starting in about thirty minutes. I was just setting up the final showcase for the groom's cake since they wanted to have two showpieces."

I stood up and leaned on my crutch, and she reached out for me before forcing herself to pull back.

That was fine. I wasn't sure what I would do if she touched me anyway.

"It looks fantastic."

She smiled then, but only part of it reached her eyes. Had I done that? Or had we done that to each other?

"I worked really hard on it. I'm glad it looks good."

"It looks better than good, Erin. You're so fucking talented."

"Thanks."

There was an awkward silence, one that I wanted to fill, but I didn't know what to say. I hated this. She had been so easy to talk to. Ever since she first walked into the bar in that sequined dress. There had never been a moment when I felt like I had to hold myself back or try too hard. Not until everything changed.

I hated it.

"It's good to see you moving around. But shouldn't you be sitting somewhere else right now?" Her words brought me out of my thoughts, and I shook my head.

"I'm fine. I was really just using the excuse to get a beer."

I felt my cheeks heat up as her brows rose.

"Really?"

"Yeah. I haven't taken a pain pill all day, but Amelia and Caleb refused to let me have a beer. It's like they're worried that I'm going to trip over myself or something. I just wanted one."

"Well, I won't tell if you don't."

She shared a conspiratorial smile with me, and it went straight to my heart—and my cock.

Hell, she would be the death of me. But what a way to go.

"I didn't know any of you guys would be here. Of course, it seems like everybody in the city of Denver is here right now."

"Yeah, it's a little ridiculous."

"But it was a beautiful wedding."

"Michael and Tony sure know how to party."

"Yes, they do."

She wrung her hands in front of her and looked down at them. "I guess I should go."

"Don't."

I hadn't known the word was going to come out of my mouth until it did. She looked up quickly, her eyes wide.

"Why?"

"Because I should have talked to you before. I shouldn't have let you go. I shouldn't have let you walk away. Damn it, I shouldn't have walked away when you asked me to that first day." I set my beer down and hobbled over to her.

She met me halfway, her face even paler than before.

"I shouldn't have left the way I did. I shouldn't have hurt you like that. I was just so scared. And making stupid decisions. And then they just compounded on each other." I leaned on one crutch and put the other one beside me on the island before reaching out to cup her face.

She was so soft under my touch, so warm. I missed this. I missed everything about her.

And I hated that I had let my anger and my issues stand in the way of us.

"You were hurting. And I could see that. But my ego was bruised, so I let myself walk away. I let you push me away."

"I shouldn't have pushed at all."

"Maybe you should have. You were the one who set the parameters of our relationship. And I was the one who wanted to change them."

"But they were stupid rules. You can't tell yourself

you're not going to fall in love." She shut her mouth quickly, her eyes widening.

"You love me?" I asked, my words a growl.

"Maybe." She said the word quickly.

"Well, maybe I love you, too."

She just stood there, blinking at me, and I really wondered how this was happening. I used to be better at words. But I sucked at this. What the fuck was wrong with me?

"I think I started to fall in love with you when I saw you in that sequined dress. But then you were married."

"And then...I wasn't."

"I don't know what happens next for us. All I know is that I've hated myself without you. I've hated the way I feel, the way I feel like I lost a limb. And it's not just the broken leg."

"I can't believe you're hurt."

"But the dog is fine. And I'm going to be fine. Seriously. But I'm not going to be one hundred percent if you're not with me. So, don't go away again, Erin. Let's work on this. Let's figure this out. Because I want to see what other cakes you can make. I want to see you smile. I want you to dance with me as soon as I can dance again. I want to go on dates with you. I just want to see where we can go. I want to love you, Erin. I want to be by your side when we're both stressed out and worried and trying to run. I want to be the one that you run to. I should have said all of this when you were in the hospital with me. But, like I said, I reacted. I said the wrong thing. You tried to apologize, and I got angry. I shouldn't have."

"You're allowed to be angry. And that's something we both need to remember. We're both allowed to have feelings. But we need to talk about them."

"I love you, Erin. I love everything about you. Your outdated pop culture references and the fact that you get angry just like I do. I love that you love my truck as much as I do."

"I do miss your truck."

Her cheeks reddened, and I knew she was thinking about exactly what we had done in that truck.

"I want to try again. I want to figure this out. And I don't want to run."

"I'm done running."

"Good."

"I love you, Devin. I didn't mean to fall for you. And maybe I shouldn't have, or maybe I should've just let myself do what needed to be done. I was just so scared of you running away, that I ran first. I made a mistake. I don't want to do that again. So, give me a second chance. Let me love you. I'll do my best to show you that I'm worth it."

I lowered my lips to hers, just a gentle caress.

"I know you're worth it, Erin. We're worth it. So, let's figure this out. Together."

And then I kissed her again, ignoring the way my sister

and brother hooted and hollered from the doorway, or how someone came in to ask about the cake. They could wait. I'd waited a lifetime for Erin.

I'd waited for what felt like eons.

But with every step, every choice made, I knew I was breathless with her.

I knew it wouldn't be easy. But we'd figure it out. Because there was no more running for us. I had been truthful when I said that I had fallen for her when I saw her in that dress. I fell in love with the fire in her eyes.

And I couldn't wait to see where she took me next.

EPILOGUE

ERIN

I ARCHED INTO HIM, MY SHOULDERS PRESSED against the wall, my back bowing.

"Harder," I gasped out, rotating my hips on his dick.

"You asked for it," he growled. And then he pumped harder. I had one hand on the wall, trying to keep myself steady so I didn't fall, the other dug into his shoulder.

He had both hands on my sides, gripping my hips and my ass, squeezing as he pumped in and out of me.

We were both naked in the middle of my living room, christening the wall that led into my kitchen.

Eventually, we were going to run out of new places to

fuck in my house and in his. And since we weren't planning to get a new home, that just meant new positions.

At least, that's what he had promised me.

"Put your hand between us if you're going to let your mind wander like that," he growled out. I whimpered.

I pulled my hand from his shoulder and put it over his mouth. He licked between my fingers.

That sent shivers down to my pussy, and I loved the way his eyes practically crossed when it contracted.

That's my man. He knew exactly what I liked and understood what we both wanted.

I slipped my hand over my belly and between us so I could spread two fingers around where his cock slid in between my folds and use my thumb to play with my clit.

We had been going at it for so long, both of us so sweaty and needy, that it only took a few quick touches before I was coming, my pussy clamping around his cock.

He shouted, pumping once, twice, and then slamming home, my back hitting the wall so hard that it rattled the pictures on either side of us.

"Jesus Christ," he growled.

"I'm pretty sure we need to check the foundation. Is this a load-bearing wall?"

"Look at you, worrying about the shape of your house after this."

"Listen to that Eric Church song. It could happen. And

remember Buffy and Spike? They totally screwed the house all the way down."

"Well, we'll figure that out. I mean, I bet if we practice enough, we could actually have the drywall falling down around us."

"I don't want that." I grinned, clenching around him again. He groaned and kissed my lips softly.

"You don't want me to fuck you hard?"

"Oh, I want that. But let's keep the house intact. We'll just have to be careful. Plus, your bones are just now healing."

"Yes, they are. Look at me, I'm having sex on two legs." He pulled me away from the wall, and I let out a squeal. I put both hands on his hips, aware that I was still on top of his cock.

This was very interesting, and I loved it.

"See? Two legs, all hands. Behold, my prowess."

I grinned, laughing. Who would have thought I would be able to laugh with him inside me? I liked this part of our relationship. Sexy, hot, and just us.

"I'm so proud. And you know what? I did just hold your prowess."

He winked. "Damn right, you did."

"Now, let me down and help me clean up because your brothers, Thea, Amelia, Zoey, Tucker, and Tobey are on their way over with my sister and her family. Dinner's going to burn."

"That's why you set it on warm," he said but reached around for the towel that we had set down at some point. He slowly slid me off his dick. We both walked over to the bathroom and quickly turned on the shower.

"By the way, that was why it was a quickie," he said. "I really don't want my family to see my ass."

"Didn't Caleb say that he had to help you shower at some point?"

"Hey. We are not talking about that. Ever."

I put my hair up and quickly washed off my body, staying out of reach of his hands. He was quick like that. For someone who had recently lost an organ and was just now regaining the ability to walk normally again, he was very fast.

"By the way," Devin said as we both toweled each other off. "Tobey might not come. He said he had a thing."

"A thing?" I asked, worried.

"A thing."

"Interesting."

"Well, you know my family. We're all about the interesting."

I shook my head and went to my tiptoes, kissing him hard.

He hadn't shaved, but he had added a little bit of conditioner to his beard earlier that day. Considering that this was our third shower of the day because we couldn't keep our hands off each other, we were getting good at that.

"I love you, Devin."

"I love you, too." He slapped my ass through my towel, and I rolled my eyes. "If we don't hurry, they really are going to see your ass," I said with a laugh.

The doorbell rang, and we both met each other's gazes, throwing our heads back and laughing.

"Well, I guess we're running late."

"No, they're just early."

"I don't really think that's the case."

"You're right, but, quick, go put on pants. And I'll go and figure out where my dress is."

"Pretty sure we left it in the kitchen."

"Fuck."

"Hey, you two, we let ourselves in," Caleb said from the living room. "And I see a pair of lace panties. I'm guessing dinner's running late."

I put my hands over my face and let out a groan.

"I don't think I can hide from them for long, can I?"

"I don't know why you let Amelia have a key," Devin growled, stuffing himself into his jeans.

"I thought it would be prudent. For emergencies."

"There's no such thing as only emergencies when it comes to my family."

"Well, I realize that now."

"Yeah, and just imagine when we're married. It'll only get worse. You're officially going to be family."

I froze, looking at him.

He stared at me, blinking quickly.

"Did you just say 'married?'"

He swallowed hard and then looked away for a bit. "Uh, forget I said that."

"You don't want to get married?" I didn't know exactly what I felt at that moment, but disappointment was rearing its little head at me.

"Can you wait until two days from now when I have the nice dinner and the champagne's out, and I get down on one knee like I planned? And you know, not when I'm sitting here half-naked, and my brother's out there, probably holding your panties?"

My hands shook, and I just looked at him. "Married. Are you asking me to marry you?"

"I'm asking you to wait for me to ask you to marry me." Devin pinched the bridge of his nose. "Dear God. I really am the worst at this. I told you that I used to be good with words. And then I met you, and I lost the ability to speak."

"That's one of the sweetest things you've ever said."

"Yeah, but I'm a fucking idiot. I was going to wait to ask you. Until it was nice. And not now."

"What did she say?" Caleb said from the other side of the door, and both Devin and I let out a sharp yelp.

"Shut up," Devin shouted.

"What? I didn't actually touch the panties. I'm not holding them. Now, did she say yes?"

"He hasn't really asked yet," I said, not knowing where the words had come from.

Devin just stared at me. Then, without words, he went down on one knee, and tears filled my eyes.

"Erin, baby. There will always be better ways to do this. Better places to be. But, here in one of the homes that I love being with you in, maybe this is the best place. I want to spend the rest of my life with you. I want to be with you. I want to watch you smile every morning, and I want to hold you in my arms when we go to bed. I want to live this crazy life of ours and try to figure out what happens next. I want you to teach me how to bake cakes and how to decorate. And I want you to make as many package jokes as you want because I know it makes you smile. I just want to be with you. Will you marry me, Erin?"

I tried to say something, but I was too busy choking out a sob to do anything else. I had never thought I would get married again. After all, I'd thought I married the person I was supposed to wed.

But Nicholas was already remarried, living his life. And I didn't love him.

I loved the man in front of me. With all of my heart.

And so, as I stood there in a towel with the love of my life—the *true* love of my life—down on one knee in front of me, no ring in his hand yet, and steam fogging up the mirror, I did the only thing I could do.

I lowered my voice, my hands shaking, and said,

"Yes."

THE END

Next in the Less Than series?

It's Amelia's turn in RECKLESS WITH YOU.

WANT TO READ A SPECIAL BONUS EPILOGUE FEATURING DEVIN & ERIN? CLICK HERE!

A Note from Carrie Ann Ryan

Thank you so much for reading **BREATHLESS WITH HER!**

I love second chances. As someone who is rebuilding her life, writing books where someone can find who they are in their new life means everything. I hope you loved Erin and Devin's book.

As for who is next? Amelia thinks she knows what she wants in Reckless With You. Just what until you see what she gets!

If you'd like to read Dimitri's romance, his story is Restless Ink!

The Less Than Series:
Book 1: Breathless With Her
Book 2: Reckless With You

Book 3: Shameless With Him

Want to read a special BONUS EPILOGUE featuring Devin & Erin? CLICK HERE!

If you want to make sure you know what's coming next from me, you can sign up for my newsletter at www.CarrieAnnRyan.com; follow me on twitter at @CarrieAnnRyan, or like my Facebook page. I also have a Facebook Fan Club where we have trivia, chats, and other goodies. You guys are the reason I get to do what I do and I thank you.

Make sure you're signed up for my MAILING LIST so you can know when the next releases are available as well as find giveaways and FREE READS.

Happy Reading!

ALSO FROM CARRIE ANN RYAN

The Montgomery Ink Legacy Series:
Book 1: Bittersweet Promises

The Wilder Brothers Series:
Book 1: One Way Back to Me
Book 2: Always the One for Me

The Aspen Pack Series:
Book 1: Etched in Honor

The Montgomery Ink: Fort Collins Series:
Book 1: Inked Persuasion
Book 2: Inked Obsession
Book 3: Inked Devotion

Book 3.5: Nothing But Ink

Book 4: Inked Craving

Book 5: Inked Temptation

The Montgomery Ink: Boulder Series:

Book 1: Wrapped in Ink

Book 2: Sated in Ink

Book 3: Embraced in Ink

Book 3: Moments in Ink

Book 4: Seduced in Ink

Book 4.5: Captured in Ink

Book 4.7: Inked Fantasy

Book 4.8: A Very Montgomery Christmas

Montgomery Ink: Colorado Springs

Book 1: Fallen Ink

Book 2: Restless Ink

Book 2.5: Ashes to Ink

Book 3: Jagged Ink

Book 3.5: Ink by Numbers

Montgomery Ink Denver:

Book 0.5: Ink Inspired

Book 0.6: Ink Reunited

Book 1: Delicate Ink

Book 1.5: Forever Ink

Book 2: Tempting Boundaries

Book 3: <u>Harder than Words</u>
Book 3.5: <u>Finally Found You</u>
Book 4: <u>Written in Ink</u>
Book 4.5: <u>Hidden Ink</u>
Book 5: <u>Ink Enduring</u>
Book 6: <u>Ink Exposed</u>
Book 6.5: <u>Adoring Ink</u>
Book 6.6: <u>Love, Honor, & Ink</u>
Book 7: <u>Inked Expressions</u>
Book 7.3: <u>Dropout</u>
Book 7.5: <u>Executive Ink</u>
Book 8: <u>Inked Memories</u>
Book 8.5: <u>Inked Nights</u>
Book 8.7: <u>Second Chance Ink</u>
Book 8.5: Montgomery Midnight Kisses
Bonus: Inked Kingdom

The On My Own Series:
Book 0.5: My First Glance
Book 1: My One Night
Book 2: My Rebound
Book 3: My Next Play
Book 4: My Bad Decisions

The Promise Me Series:
Book 1: Forever Only Once
Book 2: From That Moment

Book 3: Far From Destined

Book 4: From Our First

The Less Than Series:

Book 1: Breathless With Her

Book 2: Reckless With You

Book 3: Shameless With Him

The Fractured Connections Series:

Book 1: Breaking Without You

Book 2: Shouldn't Have You

Book 3: Falling With You

Book 4: Taken With You

The Whiskey and Lies Series:

Book 1: Whiskey Secrets

Book 2: Whiskey Reveals

Book 3: Whiskey Undone

The Gallagher Brothers Series:

Book 1: Love Restored

Book 2: Passion Restored

Book 3: Hope Restored

The Ravenwood Coven Series:

Book 1: Dawn Unearthed

Book 2: Dusk Unveiled

Book 3: Evernight Unleashed

The Talon Pack:

Book 1: Tattered Loyalties

Book 2: An Alpha's Choice

Book 3: Mated in Mist

Book 4: Wolf Betrayed

Book 5: Fractured Silence

Book 6: Destiny Disgraced

Book 7: Eternal Mourning

Book 8: Strength Enduring

Book 9: Forever Broken

Book 10: Mated in Darkness

Book 11: Fated in Winter

Redwood Pack Series:

Book 1: An Alpha's Path

Book 2: A Taste for a Mate

Book 3: Trinity Bound

Book 3.5: A Night Away

Book 4: Enforcer's Redemption

Book 4.5: Blurred Expectations

Book 4.7: Forgiveness

Book 5: Shattered Emotions

Book 6: Hidden Destiny

Book 6.5: A Beta's Haven

Book 7: Fighting Fate

Book 7.5: <u>Loving the Omega</u>
Book 7.7: <u>The Hunted Heart</u>
Book 8: <u>Wicked Wolf</u>

The Elements of Five Series:
Book 1: From Breath and Ruin
Book 2: From Flame and Ash
Book 3: From Spirit and Binding
Book 4: From Shadow and Silence

Dante's Circle Series:
Book 1: <u>Dust of My Wings</u>
Book 2: <u>Her Warriors' Three Wishes</u>
Book 3: <u>An Unlucky Moon</u>
Book 3.5: <u>His Choice</u>
Book 4: <u>Tangled Innocence</u>
Book 5: <u>Fierce Enchantment</u>
Book 6: <u>An Immortal's Song</u>
Book 7: <u>Prowled Darkness</u>
Book 8: Dante's Circle Reborn

Holiday, Montana Series:
Book 1: <u>Charmed Spirits</u>
Book 2: <u>Santa's Executive</u>
Book 3: <u>Finding Abigail</u>
Book 4: <u>Her Lucky Love</u>
Book 5: Dreams of Ivory

The Branded Pack Series:
(Written with Alexandra Ivy)
Book 1: <u>Stolen and Forgiven</u>
Book 2: <u>Abandoned and Unseen</u>
Book 3: <u>Buried and Shadowed</u>

ABOUT THE AUTHOR

Carrie Ann Ryan is the New York Times and USA Today bestselling author of contemporary, paranormal, and young adult romance. Her works include the Montgomery Ink, Redwood Pack, Fractured Connections, and Elements of Five series, which have sold over 3.0 million books worldwide. She started writing while in graduate school for her advanced degree in chemistry and hasn't stopped since.

Carrie Ann has written over seventy-five novels and novellas with more in the works. When she's not losing herself in her emotional and action-packed worlds, she's reading as much as she can while wrangling her clowder of cats who have more followers than she does.

www.CarrieAnnRyan.com